Douglas Adams created all the various and contradictory manifestations of *The Hitchhiker's Guide to the Galaxy*: radio, novels, TV, computer game, stage adaptations, comic book and bath towel. A major movie is currently in development hell and will almost certainly be released any decade now. He lectured and broadcast around the world and was a patron of the Dian Fossey Gorilla Fund and Save the Rhino International.

He was born in Cambridge, UK and lived with his wife and daughter in Santa Barbara, California, where he died suddenly on 11 May 2001.

For more information, visit *www.douglasadams.com*

If you are interested in the works of Douglas Adams, you may like to join ZZ9 Plural Z Alpha, the official Hitchhiker's Guide to the Galaxy Appreciation Society, founded in 1980. For details of this fan-run club visit www.zz9.org or send a SAE/IRC to:

ZZ9 Plural Z Alpha
4 The Sycamores, Hadfield
Derbyshire, SK13 2BS, UK

by the same author

The Hitchhiker series:

The Hitchhiker's Guide to the Galaxy
The Restaurant at the End of the Universe
Life, the Universe and Everything
So Long, and Thanks for all the Fish
Mostly Harmless
The Original Hitchhiker Radio Scripts

The Dirk Gently series:

Dirk Gently's Holistic Detective Agency
The Long Dark Tea-time of the Soul
The Salmon of Doubt

With John Lloyd:

The Meaning of Liff
The Deeper Meaning of Liff

With Mark Carwardine:

Last Chance to See . . .

By Terry Jones, based on a story/
computer game by Douglas Adams:

Starship Titanic

DOUGLAS ADAMS

Mostly Harmless

Pan Books

First published 1992 by William Heinemann Ltd

This edition published 1993 by Pan Books
an imprint of Pan Macmillan Ltd
Pan Macmillan, 20 New Wharf Road, London N1 9RR
Basingstoke and Oxford
Associated companies throughout the world
www.panmacmillan.com

In association with William Heinemann Ltd

ISBN-13: 978-0-330-32311-6
ISBN-10: 0-330-32311-3

39 41 43 45 44 42 40

A CIP catalogue record for this book is available from
the British Library.

Typeset by SetSystems Ltd, Saffron Walden, Essex
Printed and bound in Great Britain by
Mackays of Chatham plc, Chatham, Kent

for Ron

With grateful thanks to Sue Freestone
and Michael Bywater for their support,
help and constructive abuse.

Anything that happens, happens.

Anything that, in happening, causes something else to happen, causes something else to happen.

Anything that, in happening, causes
itself to happen again, happens again.

It doesn't necessarily do it
in chronological order, though.

1

The history of the Galaxy has got a little muddled, for a number of reasons: partly because those who are trying to keep track of it have got a little muddled, but also because some very muddling things have been happening anyway.

One of the problems has to do with the speed of light and the difficulties involved in trying to exceed it. You can't. Nothing travels faster than the speed of light with the possible exception of bad news, which obeys its own special laws. The Hingefreel people of Arkintoofle Minor did try to build spaceships that were powered by bad news but they didn't work particularly well and were so extremely unwelcome whenever they arrived anywhere that there wasn't really any point in being there.

So, by and large, the peoples of the Galaxy tended to languish in their own local muddles and the history of the Galaxy itself was, for a long time, largely cosmological.

Which is not to say that people weren't trying. They tried sending off fleets of spaceships to do battle or business in distant parts, but these usually took thousands of years to get anywhere. By the time they eventually arrived, other forms of travel had been discovered which made use of hyperspace to circumvent the speed of light, so that whatever battles it was that the slower-than-light fleets had been sent to fight had already been taken care of centuries earlier by the time they actually got there.

This didn't, of course, deter their crews from wanting to fight the battles anyway. They were trained, they were ready, they'd had a couple of thousand years' sleep, they'd come a long way to do a tough job and by Zarquon they were going to do it.

This was when the first major muddles of Galactic history set in, with battles continually re-erupting centuries after the issues they had been fought over had supposedly been settled. However, these muddles were as nothing to the ones which historians had to try and unravel once time-travel was discovered and battles started *pre*-erupting hundreds of years before the issues even arose. When the Infinite Improbability Drive arrived and whole planets started turning unexpectedly into banana fruitcake, the great history faculty of the University of Maximegalon finally gave up, closed itself down and surrendered its buildings to the rapidly growing joint faculty of Divinity and Water Polo, which had been after them for years.

Which is all very well, of course, but it almost certainly means that no one will ever know for sure where, for instance, the Grebulons came from, or exactly what it was they wanted. And this is a pity, because if anybody had known anything about them, it is just possible that a most terrible catastrophe would have been averted – or at least would have had to find a different way to happen.

Click, hum.

The huge grey Grebulon reconnaissance ship moved silently through the black void. It was travelling at fabulous, breathtaking speed, yet appeared, against the glimmering background of a billion distant stars, to be moving not at all. It was just one dark speck frozen against an infinite granularity of brilliant night.

On board the ship, everything was as it had been for millennia, deeply dark and silent.

Click, hum.

At least, almost everything.

Click, click, hum.

Click, hum, click, hum, click, hum.

Click, click, click, click, click, hum.

Hmmm.

A low-level supervising program woke up a slightly higher level supervising program deep in the ship's semi-somnolent cyberbrain and reported to it that whenever it went click all it got was a hum.

The higher level supervising program asked it what it was supposed to get, and the low-level supervising program said that it couldn't remember exactly, but thought it was probably more of a sort of distant satisfied sigh, wasn't it? It didn't know what this hum was. Click, hum, click, hum. That was all it was getting.

The higher level supervising program considered this and didn't like it. It asked the low-level supervising program what exactly it was supervising and the low-level supervising program said it couldn't remember that either, just that it was something that was meant to go click, sigh every ten years or so, which usually happened without fail. It had tried to consult its error look-up table but couldn't find it, which was why it had alerted the higher level supervising program to the problem.

The higher level supervising program went to consult one of its own look-up tables to find out what the low-level supervising program was meant to be supervising.

It couldn't find the look-up table.

Odd.

It looked again. All it got was an error message. It tried to look up the error message in its error message look-up table and couldn't find that either. It allowed a couple of nanoseconds to go by while it went through all this again. Then it woke up its sector function supervisor.

The sector function supervisor hit immediate problems. It called its supervising agent which hit problems too. Within a few millionths of a second virtual circuits that had lain dormant, some for years, some for centuries, were flaring into life throughout the ship. Something, somewhere, had gone terribly wrong, but none of the supervising programs could tell what it was. At every level, vital instructions were missing, and the instructions about what to do in the event of discovering that vital instructions were missing, were also missing.

Small modules of software – agents – surged through the logical pathways, grouping, consulting, re-grouping. They quickly established that the ship's memory, all the way back to its central mission module, was in tatters. No amount of interrogation could determine what it was that had happened. Even the central mission module itself seemed to be damaged.

This made the whole problem very simple to deal with. Replace the central mission module. There was another one, a backup, an exact duplicate of the original. It had to be physically replaced because, for safety reasons, there was no link whatsoever between the original and its backup. Once the central mission module was replaced it could itself supervise the reconstruction of the rest of the system in every detail, and all would be well.

Robots were instructed to bring the backup central mission module from the shielded strong room, where they guarded it, to the ship's logic chamber for installation.

This involved the lengthy exchange of emergency codes and protocols as the robots interrogated the agents as to the authenticity of the instructions. At last the robots were satisfied that all procedures were correct. They unpacked the backup central mission module from its storage housing, carried it out of the storage chamber, fell out of the ship and went spinning off into the void.

This provided the first major clue as to what it was that was wrong.

Further investigation quickly established what it was that had happened. A meteorite had knocked a large hole in the ship. The ship had not previously detected this because the meteorite had neatly knocked out that part of the ship's processing equipment which was supposed to detect if the ship had been hit by a meteorite.

The first thing to do was to try to seal up the hole. This turned out to be impossible, because the ship's sensors couldn't see that there was a hole, and the supervisors which should have said that the sensors weren't working properly weren't working properly and kept saying that the sensors were fine. The ship could only deduce the existence of the hole from the fact that the robots had clearly fallen out of it, taking its spare brain, which would have enabled it to see the hole, with them.

The ship tried to think intelligently about this, failed, and then blanked out completely for a bit. It didn't realize it had blanked out, of course, because it had blanked out. It was merely surprised to see the stars jump. After the third time the stars jumped the ship finally realized that it must be blanking out, and that it was time to take some serious decisions.

It relaxed.

Then it realized it hadn't actually taken the serious decisions yet and panicked. It blanked out again for a bit. When it awoke again it sealed all the bulkheads around where it knew the unseen hole must be.

It clearly hadn't got to its destination yet, it thought,

fitfully, but since it no longer had the faintest idea where its destination was or how to reach it, there seemed to be little point in continuing. It consulted what tiny scraps of instructions it could reconstruct from the tatters of its central mission module.

'Your !!!!! !!!!! !!!!! year mission is to !!!!! !!!!! !!!!!, !!!!!, !!!!! !!!!! !!!!! !!!!!, land !!!!! !!!!! !!!!! a safe distance !!!!! !!!!! monitor it. !!!!! !!!!! !!!!! . . .'

All of the rest was complete garbage.

Before it blanked out for good the ship would have to pass on those instructions, such as they were, to its more primitive subsidiary systems.

It must also revive all of its crew.

There was another problem. While the crew was in hibernation, the minds of all of its members, their memories, their identities and their understanding of what they had come to do, had all been transferred into the ship's central mission module for safe keeping. The crew would not have the faintest idea of who they were or what they were doing there. Oh well.

Just before it blanked out for the final time, the ship realized that its engines were beginning to give out too.

The ship and its revived and confused crew coasted on under the control of its subsidiary automatic systems, which simply looked to land wherever they could find to land and monitor whatever they could find to monitor.

As far as finding something to land on was concerned, they didn't do very well. The planet they found was desolately cold and lonely, so achingly far from the sun that should warm it, that it took all of the Envir-O-Form machinery and LifeSupport-O-Systems they carried with them to render it, or at least enough parts of it, habitable. There were better planets nearer in, but the ship's Strateej-O-Mat was obviously locked into Lurk mode and chose the most distant and unobtrusive planet and, furthermore, would not be gainsaid by anybody other than the ship's Chief Strategic Officer. Since everybody on the ship had lost their minds no one knew who the Chief Strategic Officer was or, even if he could have been identified, how he was supposed to go about gainsaying the ship's Strateej-O-Mat.

As far as finding something to monitor was concerned, though, they hit solid gold.

2

One of the extraordinary things about life is the sort of places it's prepared to put up with living. Anywhere it can get some kind of a grip, whether it's the intoxicating seas of Santraginus V, where the fish never seem to care whatever the heck kind of direction they swim in, the fire storms of Frastra where, they say, life begins at 40,000 degrees, or just burrowing around in the lower intestine of a rat for the sheer unadulterated hell of it, life will always find a way of hanging on in somewhere.

It will even live in New York, though it's hard to know why. In the winter time the temperature falls well below the legal minimum, or rather it would do if anybody had the common sense to set a legal minimum. The last time anybody made a list of the top hundred character attributes of New Yorkers, common sense snuck in at number 79.

In the summer it's too darn hot. It's one thing to be the sort of life form that thrives on heat and finds, as the Frastrans do, that the temperature range between 40,000 and 40,004 is very equable, but it's quite another to be the sort of animal that has to wrap itself up in lots of other animals at one point in your planet's orbit, and then find, half an orbit later, that your skin's bubbling.

Spring is over-rated. A lot of the inhabitants of New York will honk on mightily about the pleasures of spring, but if they actually knew the first thing about the pleasures of spring they would know of at least five thousand nine hundred and eighty-three better places to spend it than New York, and that's just on the same latitude.

Fall, though, is the worst. Few things are worse than fall in New York. Some of the things that live in the lower intestines of rats would disagree, but most of the things that live in the lower intestines of rats are highly disagreeable anyway, so their opinion can and should be discounted. When it's fall in New York, the air smells as if someone's been frying goats in it, and if you are keen to breathe, the best plan is to open a window and stick your head in a building.

Tricia McMillan loved New York. She kept on telling herself this over and over again. The Upper West Side. Yeah. Mid Town. Hey, great retail. SoHo. The East Village. Clothes. Books. Sushi. Italian. Delis. Yo.

Movies. Yo also. Tricia had just been to see Woody Allen's new movie, which was all about the angst of being neurotic in New York. He had made one or two other movies that had explored the same theme, and Tricia wondered if he had ever considered moving, but heard that he had set his face against the idea. So: more movies, she guessed.

Tricia loved New York because loving New York was a good career move. It was a good retail move, a good cuisine move, not a good taxi move or a great quality of pavement move, but definitely a career move that ranked amongst the highest and the best. Tricia was a TV anchor person, and New York was where most of the world's TV was anchored. Tricia's TV anchoring had been done exclusively in Britain up to that point: regional news, then breakfast news, early evening news. She would have been called, if the language allowed, a rapidly rising anchor, but . . . hey, this is television, what does it matter? She was a rapidly rising anchor. She had what it took: great hair, a profound understanding of strategic lip gloss, the intelligence to understand the world and a tiny secret interior deadness which meant she didn't care. Everybody has their moment of great opportunity in life. If you happen to miss the one you care about, then everything else in life becomes eerily easy.

Tricia had only ever missed one opportunity. These days it didn't even make her tremble quite so much as it used to to think about it. She guessed it was that bit of her that had gone dead.

NBS needed a new anchor. Mo Minetti was leaving the *US/AM* breakfast show to have a baby. She had been offered a mind-bubbling amount of money to have it on the show, but she had declined, unexpectedly, on grounds of personal privacy and taste. Teams of NBS lawyers had sieved through her contract to see if these constituted legitimate grounds, but in the end, reluctantly, they had to let her go. This was, for them, particularly galling because normally 'reluctantly letting someone go' was an expression that had its boot on quite another foot.

The word was out that maybe, just maybe, a British accent would fit. The hair, the skin tone and the bridgework would have to be up to American network standards, but there had been a lot of British accents up there thanking their mothers for their Oscars, a lot of British accents singing on Broadway, and some unusually big audiences tuning in to British accents in wigs on Masterpiece Theatre. British accents were telling jokes on David Letterman and Jay Leno. Nobody understood the jokes but they were really responding to the accents, so maybe it was time, just maybe. A British accent on *US/AM*. Well, hell.

That was why Tricia was here. This was why loving New York was a great career move.

It wasn't, of course, the stated reason. Her TV company back in the UK would hardly have stumped up the air fare and hotel bill for her to go job hunting in Manhattan. Since she was chasing something like ten times her present salary, they might have felt that she could have forked out her own expenses, but she'd found a story, found a pretext, kept very quiet about anything ulterior, and they'd stumped up for the trip. A business class ticket, of course, but her face was known and she'd smiled herself an upgrade. The right moves had got her a nice room at the Brentwood and here she was, wondering what to do next.

The word on the street was one thing, making contact was another. She had a couple of names, a couple of numbers, but all it took was being put on indeterminate hold a couple of times and she was back at square one. She'd put out feelers, left messages, but so far none had been returned. The actual job she had come to do she had done in a morning; the imagined job she was after was only shimmering tantalizingly on an unreachable horizon.

Shit.

She caught a cab from the movie theatre back to the Brentwood. The cab couldn't get close to the kerb because a big stretch limo was hogging all the available space and she had to squeeze her way past it. She walked out of the fetid, goat-frying air and into the blessed cool of the lobby. The fine cotton of her blouse was sticking like grime to her skin. Her hair felt as if she'd bought it at a fairground on a stick. At the front desk she asked if there were any messages, grimly expecting none. There was one.

Oh . . .

Good.

It had worked. She had gone out to the movie specifically in order to make the phone ring. She couldn't bear sitting in a hotel room waiting.

She wondered. Should she open the message down here? Her clothes were itching and she longed to take them all off and just lie on the bed. She had turned the air conditioning way down to its bottom temperature setting, way up to its top fan setting. What she wanted more than anything else in the world at the moment was goose pimples. Then a hot shower, then a cool one, then lying on a towel, on the bed again, drying in the air conditioning. Then reading the message. Maybe more goose pimples. Maybe all sorts of things.

No. What she wanted more than anything else in the world was a job in American television at ten times her current salary. More than anything else in the world. In the world. What she wanted more than anything else at all was no longer a live issue.

She sat on a chair in the lobby, under a kentia palm, and opened the little cellophane-windowed envelope.

'Please call,' it said. 'Not happy,' and gave a number. The name was Gail Andrews.

Gail Andrews.

It wasn't a name she was expecting. It caught her unawares. She recognized it, but couldn't immediately say why. Was she Andy Martin's secretary? Hilary Bass's assistant? Martin and Bass were the two major contact calls she had made, or tried to make, at NBS. And what did 'Not happy' mean?

'Not *happy*?'

She was completely bewildered. Was this Woody Allen trying to contact her under an assumed name? It was a 212 area code number. So it was someone in New York. Who was not happy. Well, that narrowed it down a bit, didn't it?

She went back to the receptionist at the desk.

'I have a problem with this message you just gave me,' she said. 'Someone I don't know has tried to call me and says she's not happy.'

The receptionist peered at the note with a frown.

'Do you know this person?' he said.

'No,' Tricia said.

'Hmmm,' said the receptionist. 'Sounds like she's not happy about something.'

'Yes,' said Tricia.

'Looks like there's a name here,' said the receptionist. 'Gail Andrews. Do you know anybody of that name?'

'No,' said Tricia.

'Any idea what she's unhappy about?'

'No,' said Tricia.

'Have you called the number? There's a number here.'

'No,' said Tricia, 'you only just gave me the note. I'm just trying to get some more information before I ring back. Perhaps I could talk to the person who took the call?'

'Hmmm,' said the receptionist, scrutinizing the note carefully. 'I don't think we have anybody called Gail Andrews here.'

'No, I realize that,' said Tricia. 'I just—'

'I'm Gail Andrews.'

The voice came from behind Tricia. She turned round.

'I'm sorry?'

'I'm Gail Andrews. You interviewed me this morning.'

'Oh. Oh good heavens yes,' said Tricia, slightly flustered.

'I left the message for you a few hours ago. I hadn't heard so I came by. I didn't want to miss you.'

'Oh. No. Of course,' said Tricia, trying hard to get up to speed.

'I don't know about this,' said the receptionist, for whom speed was not an issue. 'Would you like me to try this number for you now?'

'No, that'll be fine, thanks,' said Tricia. 'I can handle it now.'

'I can call this room number here for you if that'll help,' said the receptionist, peering at the note again.

'No, that won't be necessary, thanks,' said Tricia. 'That's my own room number. I'm the one the message was for. I think we've sorted this out now.'

'You have a nice day now,' said the receptionist.

Tricia didn't particularly want to have a nice day. She was busy.

She also didn't want to talk to Gail Andrews. She had a very strict cut-off point as far as fraternizing with the Christians was concerned. Her colleagues called her interview subjects Christians and would often cross themselves when they saw one walking innocently into the studio to face Tricia, particularly if Tricia was smiling warmly and showing her teeth.

She turned and smiled frostily, wondering what to do.

Gail Andrews was a well-groomed woman in her mid-forties. Her clothes fell within the boundaries defined by expensive good taste, but were definitely huddled up at the floatier end of those boundaries. She was an astrologer – a famous and, if rumour were true, influential astrologer, having allegedly influenced a number of decisions made by the late President Hudson, including everything from which flavour of cream whip to have on which day of the week, to whether or not to bomb Damascus.

Tricia had savaged her more than somewhat. Not on the grounds of whether or not the stories about the

President were true, that was old hat now. At the time Ms Andrews had emphatically denied advising President Hudson on anything other than personal, spiritual or dietary matters, which did not, apparently include the bombing of Damascus. ('NOTHING PERSONAL, DAMASCUS!' the tabloids had hooted at the time.)

No, this was a neat topical little angle that Tricia had come up with about the whole issue of astrology itself. Ms Andrews had not been entirely ready for it. Tricia, on the other hand, was not entirely ready for a re-match in the hotel lobby. What to do?

'I can wait for you in the bar, if you need a few minutes,' said Gail Andrews. 'But I would like to talk to you, and I'm leaving the city tonight.'

She seemed to be slightly anxious about something rather than aggrieved or irate.

'OK,' said Tricia. 'Give me ten minutes.'

She went up to her room. Apart from anything else, she had so little faith in the ability of the guy on the message desk at reception to deal with anything as complicated as a message that she wanted to be doubly certain that there wasn't a note under the door. It wouldn't be the first time that messages at the desk and messages under the door had been completely at odds with each other.

There wasn't one.

The message light on the phone was flashing, though.

She hit the message button and got the hotel operator.

'You have a message from Gary Andress,' said the operator.

'Yes?' said Tricia. An unfamiliar name. 'What does it say.'

'Not hippy,' said the operator.

'Not *what*?' said Tricia.

'Hippy. What it says. Guy says he's not a hippy. I

guess he wanted you to know that. You want the number?'

As she started to dictate the number Tricia suddenly realized that this was just a garbled version of the message she had already had.

'OK, OK,' she said. 'Are there any other messages for me?'

'Room number?'

Tricia couldn't work out why the operator should suddenly ask for her number this late in the conversation, but gave it to her anyway.

'Name?'

'McMillan, Tricia McMillan.' Tricia spelt it, patiently.

'Not Mr MacManus?'

'No.'

'No more messages for you.' Click.

Tricia sighed and dialled again. This time she gave her name and room number all over again, up front. The operator showed not the slightest glimmer of recognition that they had been speaking less than ten seconds ago.

'I'm going to be in the bar,' Tricia explained. 'In the bar. If a phone call comes through for me, please would you put it through to me in the bar?'

'Name?'

They went through it all a couple more times till Tricia was certain that everything that possibly could be clear was as clear as it possibly could be.

She showered, put on fresh clothes and retouched her makeup with the speed of a professional, and, looking at her bed with a sigh, left the room again.

She had half a mind just to sneak off and hide.

No. Not really.

She had a look at herself in the mirror in the elevator lobby while she was waiting. She looked cool and in charge, and if she could fool herself she could fool anybody.

She was just going to have to tough it out with Gail Andrews. OK, she had given her a hard time. Sorry but that's the game we're all in – that sort of thing. Ms Andrews had agreed to do the interview because she had a new book out and TV exposure was free publicity. But there's no such thing as a free launch. No, she edited that line out again.

What had happened was this:

Last week astronomers had announced that they had at last discovered a tenth planet, out beyond the orbit of Pluto. They had been searching for it for years, guided by certain orbital anomalies in the outer planets, and now they'd found it and they were all terribly pleased, and everyone was terribly happy for them and so on. The planet was named Persephone, but rapidly nicknamed Rupert after some astronomer's parrot – there was some tediously heart-warming story attached to this – and that was all very wonderful and lovely.

Tricia had followed the story with, for various reasons, considerable interest.

Then, while she had been casting around for a good excuse to go to New York at her TV company's expense she had happened to notice a press release about Gail Andrews, and her new book, *You and Your Planets*.

Gail Andrews was not exactly a household name, but the moment you mentioned President Hudson, cream whips and the amputation of Damascus (the world had moved on from surgical strikes. The official term had in fact been 'Damascectomy', meaning the 'taking out' of Damascus), everyone remembered who you meant.

Tricia saw an angle here which she quickly sold to her producer.

Surely the notion that great lumps of rock whirling in space knew something about your day that you didn't must take a bit of a knock from the fact that there was suddenly a new lump of rock out there that nobody had known about before.

That must throw a few calculations out, mustn't it?

What about all those star charts and planetary motions and so? We all knew (apparently) what happened when Neptune was in Virgo, and so on, but what about when Rupert was rising? Wouldn't the whole of astrology have to be rethought? Wouldn't now perhaps be a good time to own up that it was all just a load of hogwash and instead take up pig-farming, the principles of which were founded on some kind of rational basis? If we'd known about Rupert three years ago, might President Hudson have been eating the boysenberry flavour on Thursday rather than Friday? Might Damascus still be standing? That sort of thing.

Gail Andrews had taken it all reasonably well. She was just starting to recover from the initial onslaught, when she made the rather serious mistake of trying to shake Tricia off by talking smoothly about diurnal arcs, right ascensions and some of the more abstruse areas of three-dimensional trigonometry.

To her shock she discovered that everything she delivered to Tricia came right back at her with more spin on it than she could cope with. Nobody had warned Gail that being a TV bimbo was, for Tricia, her second stab at a role in life. Behind her Chanel lip gloss, her *coupe sauvage* and her crystal blue contact lenses lay a brain that had acquired for itself, in an earlier, abandoned phase of her life, a first-class degree in mathematics and a doctorate in astrophysics.

As she was getting into the elevator Tricia, slightly preoccupied, realized she had left her bag in her room and wondered whether to duck back out and get it. No. It was probably safer where it was and there wasn't anything she particularly needed in it. She let the door close behind her.

Besides, she told herself, taking a deep breath, if life had taught her anything it was this:

Never go back for your bag.

As the elevator went down she stared up at the ceiling in a rather intent way. Anyone who didn't know Tricia McMillan better would have said that that was exactly the way people sometimes stared upwards when they were trying to hold back tears. She must have been staring at the tiny security video camera mounted up in the corner.

She marched rather briskly out of the elevator a minute later, and went up to the reception desk again.

'Now, I'm going to write this out,' she said, 'because I don't want anything to go wrong.'

She wrote her name in large letters on a piece of paper, then her room number, then 'IN THE BAR' and gave it to the receptionist, who looked at it.

'That's in case there's a message for me. OK?'

The receptionist continued to look at it.

'You want me to see if she's in her room?' he said.

Two minutes later, Tricia swivelled into the bar seat next to Gail Andrews, who was sitting in front of a glass of white wine.

'You struck me as the sort of person who preferred to sit up at the bar rather than demurely at a table,' she said.

This was true, and caught Tricia a little by surprise.

'Vodka?' said Gail.

'Yes,' said Tricia, suspiciously. She just stopped herself asking, 'How did you know?' but Gail answered anyway.

'I asked the barman,' she said, with a kindly smile.

The barman had her vodka ready for her and did it charmingly across the glossy mahogany.

'Thank you,' said Tricia, stirring it sharply.

She didn't know quite what to make out of all this sudden niceness and was determined not to be wrong-footed by it. People in New York were not nice to each other without reason.

'Ms Andrews,' she said, firmly, 'I'm sorry that you're not happy. I know you probably feel I was a bit rough with you this morning, but astrology is, after all, just popular entertainment, which is fine. It's part of show-biz and it's a part that you have done well out of and good luck to you. It's fun. It's not a science, though, and it shouldn't be mistaken for one. I think that's something we both managed to demonstrate very successfully together this morning, while at the same time generating some popular entertainment, which is what we both do for a living. I'm sorry if you have a problem with that.'

'I'm perfectly happy,' said Gail Andrews.

'Oh,' said Tricia, not quite certain what to make of this. 'It said in your message that you were not happy.'

'No,' said Gail Andrews. 'I said in my message that I thought *you* were not happy, and I was just wondering why.'

Tricia felt as if she had been kicked in the back of the head. She blinked.

'*What?*' she said quietly.

'To do with the stars. You seemed very angry and unhappy about something to do with stars and planets when we were having our discussion, and it's been bothering me, which is why I came to see if you were all right.'

Tricia stared at her. 'Ms Andrews—' she started, and

then realized that the way she had said it sounded exactly angry and unhappy and rather undermined the protest she had been trying to make.

'Please call me Gail, if that's OK.'

Tricia just looked bewildered.

'*I* know that astrology isn't a science,' said Gail. 'Of course it isn't. It's just an arbitrary set of rules like chess or tennis or, what's that strange thing you British play?'

'Er, cricket? Self-loathing?'

'Parliamentary democracy. The rules just kind of got there. They don't make any kind of sense except in terms of themselves. But when you start to exercise those rules, all sorts of processes start to happen and you start to find out all sorts of stuff about people. In astrology the rules happen to be about stars and planets, but they could be about ducks and drakes for all the difference it would make. It's just a way of thinking about a problem which lets the shape of that problem begin to emerge. The more rules, the tinier the rules, the more arbitrary they are, the better. It's like throwing a handful of fine graphite dust on a piece of paper to see where the hidden indentations are. It lets you see the words that were written on the piece of paper above it that's now been taken away and hidden. The graphite's not important. It's just the means of revealing their indentations. So you see, astrology's nothing to do with astronomy. It's just to do with people thinking about people.

'So when you got so, I don't know, so emotionally *focused* on stars and planets this morning, I began to think, she's not angry about astrology, she really is angry and unhappy about actual stars and planets. People usually only get that unhappy and angry when they've lost something. That's all I could think and I couldn't make any more sense of it than that. So I came to see if you were OK.'

Tricia was stunned.

One part of her brain had already got started on all sorts of stuff. It was busy constructing all sorts of rebuttals to do with how ridiculous newspaper horoscopes were and the sort of statistical tricks they played on people. But gradually it petered out, because it realized that the rest of her brain wasn't listening. She had been completely stunned.

She had just been told, by a total stranger, something she'd kept completely secret for seventeen years.

She turned to look at Gail.

'I . . .'

She stopped.

A tiny security camera up behind the bar had turned to follow her movement. This completely flummoxed her. Most people would not have noticed it. It was not designed to be noticed. It was not designed to suggest that nowadays even an expensive and elegant hotel in New York couldn't be sure that its clientele wasn't suddenly going to pull a gun or not wear a tie. But carefully hidden though it was behind the vodka, it couldn't deceive the finely honed instinct of a TV anchor person, which was to know exactly when a camera was turning to look at her.

'Is something wrong?' asked Gail.

'No, I . . . I have to say that you've rather astonished me,' said Tricia. She decided to ignore the security camera. It was just her imagination playing tricks with her because she had television so much on her mind today. It wasn't the first time it had happened. A traffic monitoring camera, she was convinced, had swung round to follow her as she walked past it, and a security camera in Bloomingdales had seemed to make a particular point of watching her trying on hats. She was obviously going dotty. She had even imagined that a bird in Central Park had been peering at her rather intently.

She decided to put it out of her mind and took a sip of her vodka. Someone was walking round the bar asking people if they were Mr MacManus.

'OK,' she said, suddenly blurting it out. 'I don't know how you worked it out, but . . .'

'I didn't work it out, as you put it. I just listened to what you were saying.'

'What I lost, I think, was a whole other life.'

'Everybody does that. Every moment of every day. Every single decision we make, every breath we draw, opens some doors and closes many others. Most of them we don't notice. Some we do. Sounds like you noticed one.'

'Oh yes, I noticed,' said Tricia. 'All right. Here it is. It's very simple. Many years ago I met a guy at a party. He said he was from another planet and did I want to go along with him. I said, yes, OK. It was that kind of party. I said to him to wait while I went to get my bag and then I'd be happy to go off to another planet with him. He said I wouldn't need my bag. I said he obviously came from a very backward planet or he'd know that a woman always needed to take her bag with her. He got a bit impatient, but I wasn't going to be a complete pushover just because he said he was from another planet.

'I went upstairs. Took me a while to find my bag, and then there was someone else in the bathroom. Came down and he was gone.'

Tricia paused.

'And . . .?' said Gail.

'The garden door was open. I went outside. There were lights. Some kind of gleaming thing. I was just in time to see it rise up into the sky, shoot silently up through the clouds and disappear. That was it. End of story. End of one life, beginning of another. But hardly a moment of this life goes by that I don't wonder about some other me. A me that didn't go back for her bag. I feel like she's out there somewhere and I'm walking in her shadow.'

A member of the hotel staff was now going round the bar asking people if they were Mr Miller. Nobody was.

'You really think this ... person was from another planet?' asked Gail.

'Oh, certainly. There was the spacecraft. Oh, and also he had two heads.'

'*Two?* Didn't anybody else notice?'

'It was a fancy dress party.'

'I see ...'

'And he had a bird cage over it, of course. With a cloth over the cage. Pretended he had a parrot. He tapped on the cage and it did a lot of stupid "Pretty Polly" stuff and squawking and so on. Then he pulled the cloth back for a moment and roared with laughter. There was another head in there, laughing along with him. It was a worrying moment, I can tell you.'

'I think you probably did the right thing, dear, don't you?' said Gail.

'No,' said Tricia. 'No, I don't. And I couldn't carry on doing what I was doing either. I was an astrophysicist, you see. You can't be an astrophysicist properly if you've actually met someone from another planet who's got a second head that pretends to be a parrot. You just can't do it. I couldn't, at least.'

'I can see it would be hard. And that's probably why you tend to be a little hard on other people who talk what sounds like complete nonsense.'

'Yes,' said Tricia. 'I expect you're right. I'm sorry.'

'That's OK.'

'You're the first person I've ever told this, by the way.'

'I wondered. You married?'

'Er, no. So hard to tell these days, isn't it? But you're

right to ask because that was probably the reason. I came very close a few times, mostly because I wanted to have a kid. But every guy ended up asking why I was constantly looking over his shoulder. What do you tell someone? At one point I even thought I might just go to a sperm bank and take pot luck. Have somebody's child at random.'

'You can't seriously do that, can you?'

Tricia laughed. 'Probably not. I never quite went and found out for real. Never quite did it. Story of my life. Never quite did the real thing. That's why I'm in television I guess. Nothing is real.'

'Excuse me, lady, your name Tricia McMillan?'

Tricia looked round in surprise. There was a man standing there in a chauffeur's hat.

'Yes,' she said, instantly pulling herself back together again.

'Lady, I been looking for you for about an hour. Hotel said they didn't have anybody of that name, but I checked back with Mr Martin's office and they said that this was definitely where you staying. So I ask again, they still say they never heard of you, so I get them to page you anyway and they can't find you. In the end I get the office to fax a picture of you through to the car and have a look myself.'

He looked at his watch.

'May be a bit late now, but do you want to go anyway?'

Tricia was stunned.

'Mr Martin? You mean Andy Martin at NBS?'

'That's correct, lady. Screen test for *US/AM*.'

Tricia shot up out of her seat. She couldn't even bear to think of all the messages she'd heard for Mr MacManus and Mr Miller.

'Only we have to hurry,' said the chauffeur. 'As I heard it Mr Martin thinks it might be worth trying a

British accent. His boss at the network is dead against the idea. That's Mr Zwingler, and I happen to know he's flying out to the coast this evening because I'm the one has to pick him up and take him to the airport.'

'OK,' said Tricia, 'I'm ready. Let's go.'

'OK, lady. It's the big limo out the front.'

Tricia turned back to Gail. 'I'm sorry,' she said.

'Go! Go!' said Gail. 'And good luck. I've enjoyed meeting you.'

Tricia made to reach for her bag for some cash.

'Damn,' she said. She'd left it upstairs.

'Drinks are on me,' insisted Gail. 'Really. It's been very interesting.'

Tricia sighed.

'Look, I'm really sorry about this morning and . . .'

'Don't say another word. I'm fine. It's only astrology. It's harmless. It's not the end of the world.'

'Thanks.' On an impulse Tricia gave her a hug.

'You got everything?' said the chauffeur. 'You don't want to pick up your bag or anything?'

'If there's one thing that life's taught me,' said Tricia, 'it's never go back for your bag.'

Just a little over an hour later, Tricia sat on one of the pair of beds in her hotel room. For a few minutes she didn't move. She just stared at her bag, which was sitting innocently on top of the other bed.

In her hand was a note from Gail Andrews, saying, 'Don't be too disappointed. Do ring if you want to talk about it. If I were you I'd stay in at home tomorrow night. Get some rest. But don't mind me, and don't worry. It's only astrology. It's not the end of the world. Gail.'

The chauffeur had been dead right. In fact the chauffeur seemed to know more about what was going on inside NBS than any other single person she had encountered in the organization. Martin had been keen, Zwingler had not. She had had her one shot at proving Martin right and she had blown it.

Oh well. Oh well, oh well, oh well.

Time to go home. Time to phone the airline and see if she could still get the red-eye back to Heathrow tonight. She reached for the big phone directory.

Oh. First things first.

She put down the directory again, picked up her handbag, and took it through to the bathroom. She put it down and took out the small plastic case which held her contact lenses, without which she had been unable properly to read either the script or the autocue.

As she dabbed each tiny plastic cup into her eyes she reflected that if there was one thing life had taught her it was that there are times when you do not go back for your bag and other times when you do. It had yet to teach her to distinguish between the two types of occasion.

3

The Hitchhiker's Guide to the Galaxy has, in what we laughingly call the past, had a great deal to say on the subject of parallel universes. Very little of this is, however, at all comprehensible to anyone below the level of Advanced God, and since it is now well established that all known gods came into existence a good three-millionths of a second after the Universe began rather than, as they usually claimed, the previous week, they already have a great deal of explaining to do as it is, and are therefore not available for comment on matters of deep physics at this time.

One encouraging thing the *Guide* does have to say on the subject of parallel universes is that you don't stand the remotest chance of understanding it. You can therefore say 'What?' and 'Eh?' and even go cross-eyed and start to blither if you like without any fear of making a fool of yourself.

The first thing to realize about parallel universes, the *Guide* says, is that they are not parallel.

It is also important to realize that they are not, strictly speaking, universes either, but it is easiest if you try and realize that a little later, after you've realized that everything you've realized up to that moment is not true.

The reason they are not universes is that any given universe is not actually a *thing* as such, but is just a way of looking at what is technically known as the WSOGMM, or Whole Sort of General Mish Mash. The Whole Sort of General Mish Mash doesn't actually exist either, but is just the sum total of all the different ways there would be of looking at it if it did.

The reason they are not parallel is the same reason that the sea is not parallel. It doesn't mean anything. You can slice the Whole Sort of General Mish Mash any way you like and you will generally come up with something that someone will call home.

Please feel free to blither now.

The Earth with which we are here concerned, because of its particular orientation in the Whole Sort of General Mish Mash, was hit by a neutrino that other Earths were not.

A neutrino is not a big thing to be hit by.

In fact it's hard to think of anything much smaller by which one could reasonably hope to be hit. And it's not as if being hit by neutrinos was in itself a particularly unusual event for something the size of the Earth. Far from it. It would be an unusual nanosecond in which the Earth was not hit by several billion passing neutrinos.

It all depends on what you mean by 'hit', of course, seeing as matter consists almost entirely of nothing at all. The chances of a neutrino actually hitting something as it travels through all this howling emptiness are roughly comparable to that of dropping a ball bearing at random from a cruising 747 and hitting, say, an egg sandwich.

Anyway, this neutrino hit something. Nothing terribly important in the scale of things, you might say. But the problem with saying something like that is that you would be talking cross-eyed badger spit. Once something actually happens somewhere in something as wildly complicated as the Universe, Kevin knows where it will all end up – where 'Kevin' is any random entity that doesn't know nothin' about nothin'.

This neutrino struck an atom.

The atom was part of a molecule. The molecule was part of a nucleic acid. The nucleic acid was part of a gene. The gene was part of a genetic recipe for growing . . . and so on. The upshot was that a plant ended up growing an extra leaf. In Essex. Or what would, after a lot of palaver and local difficulties of a geological nature, become Essex.

The plant was a clover. It threw its weight, or rather its seed, around extremely effectively and rapidly became the world's dominant type of clover. The precise causal connection between this tiny biological happenstance and a few other minor variations that exist in that slice of the Whole Sort of General Mish Mash – such as Tricia McMillan failing to leave with Zaphod Beeblebrox, abnormally low sales of pecan-flavoured ice cream and the fact that the Earth on which all this occurred did not get demolished by the Vogons to make way for a new hyperspace bypass – is currently sitting at number 4,763,984,132 on the research project priority list at what was once the History Department of the University of Maximegalon, and no one currently at the prayer meeting by the poolside appears to feel any sense of urgency about the problem.

4

Tricia began to feel that the world was conspiring against her. She knew that this was a perfectly normal way to feel after an overnight flight going east, when you suddenly have a whole other mysteriously threatening day to deal with for which you are not the least bit prepared. But still.

There were marks on her lawn.

She didn't really care about marks on her lawn very much. Marks on her lawn could go and take a running jump as far as she was concerned. It was Saturday morning. She had just got home from New York feeling tired, crabby and paranoid, and all she wanted to do was go to bed with the radio on quietly and gradually fall asleep to the sound of Ned Sherrin being terribly clever about something.

But Eric Bartlett was not going to let her get away with not making a thorough inspection of the marks. Eric was the old gardener who came in from the village on Saturday mornings to poke around at her garden with a stick. He didn't believe in people coming in from New York first thing in the morning. Didn't hold with it. Went against nature. He believed in virtually everything else, though.

'Probably them space aliens,' he said, bending over and prodding at the edges of the small indentations with his stick. 'Hear a lot about space aliens these days. I expect it's them.'

'Do you?' said Tricia, looking furtively at her watch. Ten minutes, she reckoned. Ten minutes she'd be able to stay standing up. Then she would simply keel over, whether she was in her bedroom or still out here in the garden. That was if she just had to stand. If she also had to nod intelligently and say 'Do you?' from time to time, it might cut it down to five.

'Oh yes,' said Eric. 'They come down here, land on your lawn, and then buzz off again, sometimes with your cat. Mrs Williams at the Post Office, her cat – you know, the ginger one? – it got abducted by space aliens. Course, they brought it back the next day but it were in a very odd mood. Kept prowling around all morning, and then falling asleep in the afternoon. Used to be the other way round, is the point. Sleep in the morning, prowl in the afternoon. Jet lag, you see, from being in an interplanetary craft.'

'I see,' said Tricia.

'They dyed it tabby, too, she says. These marks are exactly the sort of marks that their landing pods would probably make.'

'You don't think it's the lawn mower?' asked Tricia.

'If the marks were more round, I'd say, but these are just off-round, you see. Altogether more alien in shape.'

'It's just that you mentioned the lawn mower was playing up and needed fixing or it might start gouging holes in the lawn.'

'I did say that, Miss Tricia, and I stand by what I said. I'm not saying it's not the lawn mower for definite, I'm just saying what seems to me more likely given the shapes of the holes. They come in over these trees, you see, in their landing pods . . .'

'Eric . . .' said Tricia, patiently.

'Tell you what, though, Miss Tricia,' said Eric, 'I will

take a look at the mower, like I meant to last week, and leave you to get on with whatever you're wanting to.'

'Thank you, Eric,' said Tricia. 'I'm going to bed now, in fact. Help yourself to anything you want in the kitchen.'

'Thank you, Miss Tricia, and good luck to you,' said Eric. He bent over and picked something from the lawn.

'There,' he said. 'Three-leaf clover. Good luck, you see.'

He peered at it closely to check that it was a real three-leaf clover and not just a regular four-leaf one that one of the leaves had fallen off. 'If I were you, though, I'd watch for signs of alien activity in the area.' He scanned the horizon keenly. 'Particularly from over there in the Henley direction.'

'Thank you, Eric,' said Tricia again. 'I will.'

She went to bed and dreamt fitfully of parrots and other birds. In the afternoon she got up and prowled around restlessly, not certain what to do with the rest of the day, or indeed the rest of her life. She spent at least an hour dithering, trying to make up her mind whether to head up into town and go to Stavro's for the evening. This was the currently fashionable spot for high-flying media people, and seeing a few friends there might help her ease herself back into the swing of things. She decided at last she would go. It was good. It was fun there. She was very fond of Stavro himself, who was a Greek with a German father – a fairly odd combination. Tricia had been to the Alpha a couple of nights earlier, which was Stavro's original club in New York, now run by his brother Karl, who thought of himself as a German with a Greek mother. Stavro would be very happy to be told that Karl was making a bit of a pig's ear of running the New York club, so Tricia would go and make him happy. There was little love lost between Stavro and Karl Mueller.

OK. That's what she would do.

She then spent another hour dithering about what to wear. At last she settled on a smart little black dress she'd got in New York. She phoned a friend to see who was likely to be at the club that evening, and was told that it was closed this evening for a private wedding party.

She thought that trying to live life according to any plan you actually work out is like trying to buy ingredients for a recipe from the supermarket. You get one of those trolleys which simply will not go in the direction you push it and end up just having to buy completely different stuff. What do you do with it? What do you do with the recipe? She didn't know.

Anyway, that night an alien spacecraft landed on her lawn.

5

She watched it coming in from over the Henley direction with mild curiosity at first, wondering what those lights were. Living, as she did, not a million miles from Heathrow, she was used to seeing lights in the sky. Not usually so late in the evening, or so low, though, which was why she was mildly curious.

When whatever it was began to come closer and closer her curiosity began to turn to bemusement.

'Hmmm,' she thought, which was about as far as she could get with thinking. She was still feeling dopey and jet-lagged and the messages that one part of her brain was busy sending to another were not necessarily arriving on time or the right way up. She left the kitchen where she'd been fixing herself a coffee and went to open the back door which led out to the garden. She took a deep breath of cool evening air, stepped outside and looked up.

There was something roughly the size of a large camper van parked about a hundred feet above her lawn.

It was really there. Hanging there. Almost silent.

Something moved deep inside her.

Her arms dropped slowly down to her side. She didn't notice the scalding coffee slopping over her foot. She was hardly breathing as slowly, inch by inch, foot by foot, the craft came downwards. Its lights were playing softly over the ground as if probing and feeling it. They played over her.

It seemed beyond all hope that she should be given her chance again. Had he found her? Had he come back?

The craft dropped down and down until at last it had settled quietly on her lawn. It didn't look exactly like the one she had seen departing all those years ago, she thought, but flashing lights in the night sky are hard to resolve into clear shapes.

Silence.

Then a click and a hum.

Then another click and another hum. Click hum, click hum.

A doorway slid open, spilling light towards her across the lawn.

She waited, tingling.

A figure stood silhouetted in the light, then another, and another.

Wide eyes blinked slowly at her. Hands were slowly raised in greeting.

'McMillan?' a voice said at last, a strange, thin voice that managed the syllables with difficulty. 'Tricia McMillan. *Ms* Tricia McMillan?'

'Yes,' said Tricia, almost soundlessly.

'We have been monitoring you.'

'M . . . monitoring? *Me?*'

'Yes.'

They looked at her for a while, their large eyes moving up and down her very slowly.

'You look smaller in real life,' one said at last.

'What?' said Tricia.

'Yes.'

'I . . . I don't understand,' said Tricia. She hadn't expected any of this, of course, but even for something she hadn't expected to begin with it wasn't going the way she expected. At last she said, 'Are you . . . are you from . . . Zaphod?'

This question seemed to cause a little consternation among the three figures. They conferred with each other in some skittering language of their own and then turned back to her.

'We don't think so. Not as far as we know,' said one.

'Where is Zaphod?' said another, looking up into the night sky.

'I . . . I don't know,' said Tricia, helplessly.

'Is it far from here? Which direction? We don't know.'

Tricia realized with a sinking heart that they had no idea who she was talking about. Or even what she was talking about. And she had no idea what they were talking about. She put her hopes tightly away again and snapped her brain back into gear. There was no point in being disappointed. She had to wake up to the fact that she had here the journalistic scoop of the century. What should she do? Go back into the house for a video camera? Wouldn't they just be gone when she got back? She was thoroughly confused as to strategy. Keep 'em talking, she thought. Figure it out later.

'You've been monitoring . . . *me*?'

'All of you. Everything on your planet. TV. Radio. Telecommunications. Computers. Video circuitry. Warehouses.'

'What?'

'Car parks. Everything. We monitor everything.'

Tricia stared at them.

'That must be very boring, isn't it?' she blurted out.

'Yes.'

'So why . . .'

'Except . . .'

'Yes? Except what?'

'Game shows. We quite like game shows.'

There was a terribly long silence as Tricia looked at the aliens and the aliens looked at her.

'There's something I would just like to get from indoors,' said Tricia very deliberately. 'Tell you what. Would you, or one of you, like to come inside with me and have a look?'

'Very much,' they all said, enthusiastically.

All three of them stood, slightly awkwardly in her sitting room, as she hurried around picking up a video camera, a 35mm camera, a tape recorder, every recording medium she could grab hold of. They were all thin and, under domestic lighting conditions, a sort of dim purplish green.

'I really won't be a second, guys,' Tricia said, as she rummaged through some drawers for spare tapes and films.

The aliens were looking at the shelves that held her CDs and her old records. One of them nudged one of the others very slightly.

'Look,' he said. 'Elvis.'

Tricia stopped, and stared at them all over again.

'You like Elvis?' she said.

'Yes,' they said.

'Elvis *Presley*?'

'Yes.'

She shook her head in bewilderment as she tried to stuff a new tape into her video camera.

'Some of your people,' said one of her visitors, hesitantly, 'think that Elvis has been kidnapped by space aliens.'

'*What?*' said Tricia. 'Has he?'

'It is possible.'

'Are you telling me that *you* have kidnapped Elvis?' gasped Tricia. She was trying to keep cool enough not to foul up her equipment, but this was all almost too much for her.

'No. Not us,' said her guests. 'Aliens. It is a very interesting possibility. We talk of it often.'

'I must get this down,' Tricia muttered to herself. She checked her video was properly loaded and working now. She pointed the camera at them. She didn't put it up to her eye because she didn't want to freak them out. But she was sufficiently experienced to be able to shoot accurately from the hip.

'OK,' she said. 'Now tell me slowly and carefully who you are. You first,' she said to the one on the left. 'What's your name?'

'I don't know.'

'You don't know?'

'No.'

'I see,' said Tricia. 'And what about you other two?'

'We don't know.'

'Good. OK. Perhaps you can tell me where you are from?'

They shook their heads.

'You don't know where you're from?'

They shook their heads again.

'So,' said Tricia. 'What are you . . . er . . .'

She was floundering but, being a professional, kept the camera steady while she did it.

'We are on a mission,' said one of the aliens.

'A *mission*? A mission to do what?'

'We do not know.'

Still she kept the camera steady.

'So what are you doing here on Earth, then?'

'We have come to fetch you.'

Rock steady, rock steady. Could have been on a tripod. She wondered if she should be using a tripod, in fact. She wondered that because it gave her a moment or two to digest what they had just said. No, she thought, hand-held gave her more flexibility. She also thought, *help*, what am I going to do?

'Why,' she asked, calmly, 'have you come to fetch me?'

'Because we have lost our minds.'

'Excuse me,' said Tricia, 'I'm going to have to get a tripod.'

They seemed happy enough to stand there doing nothing while Tricia quickly found a tripod and mounted the camera on it. Her face was completely immobile, but she did not have the faintest idea what was going on or what to think about it.

'OK,' she said, when she was ready. 'Why . . .'

We liked your interview with the astrologer.'

'You *saw* it?'

'We see everything. We are very interested in astrology. We like it. It is very interesting. Not everything is interesting. Astrology is interesting. What the stars tell us. What the stars foretell. We could do with some information like that.'

'But . . .'

Tricia didn't know where to start.

Own up, she thought. There's no point in trying to second guess any of this stuff.

So she said, 'But I don't know anything about astrology.'

'We do.'

'You do?'

'Yes. We follow our horoscopes. We are very avid. We see all your newspapers and your magazines and are very avid with them. But our leader says we have a problem.'

'You have a *leader*?'

'Yes.'

'What's his name?'

'We do not know.'

'What does he *say* his name is, for Christ's sake? Sorry, I'll need to edit that. What does he say his name is?'

'He does not know.'

'So how do you all know he's the leader?'

'He seized control. He said someone has to do something round here.'

'Ah!' said Tricia, seizing on a clue. 'Where is "here"?'

'Rupert.'

'What?'

'Your people call it Rupert. The tenth planet from your sun. We have settled there for many years. It is highly cold and uninteresting there. But good for monitoring.'

'Why are you monitoring us?'

'It is all we know to do.'

'OK,' said Tricia. 'Right. What is the problem that your leader says you have?'

'Triangulation.'

'I beg your pardon?'

'Astrology is a very precise science. We know this.'

'Well . . .' said Tricia, then left it at that.

'But it is precise for you here on Earth.'

'Ye . . . e . . . s . . .' She had a horrible feeling she was getting a vague glimmering of something.

'So when Venus is rising in Capricorn, for instance, that is from Earth. How does that work if we are out on Rupert? What if the Earth is rising in Capricorn? It is hard for us to know. Amongst the things we have forgotten, which we think are many and profound, is trigonometry.'

'Let me get this straight,' said Tricia. 'You want me to come with you to . . . Rupert . . .'

'Yes.'

'To recalculate your *horoscopes* for you to take account of the relative positions of Earth and Rupert?'

'Yes.'

'Do I get an exclusive?'

'Yes.'

'I'm your girl,' said Tricia, thinking that at the very least she could sell it to the *National Enquirer*.

As she boarded the craft that would take her off to the furthest limits of the solar system, the first thing that met her eyes was a bank of video monitors across which thousands of images were sweeping. A fourth alien was sitting watching them, but was focused on one particular screen that held a steady image. It was a replay of the impromptu interview which Tricia had just conducted with his three colleagues. He looked up when he saw her apprehensively climbing in.

'Good evening, Ms McMillan,' he said. 'Nice camera work.'

6

Ford Prefect hit the ground running. The ground was about three inches further from the ventilation shaft than he remembered it so he misjudged the point at which he would hit the ground, started running too soon, stumbled awkwardly and twisted his ankle. Damn! He ran off down the corridor anyway, hobbling slightly.

All over the building, alarms were erupting into their usual frenzy of excitement. He dived for cover behind the usual storage cabinets, glanced around to check that he was unseen, and started rapidly to fish around inside his satchel for the usual things he needed.

His ankle, unusually, was hurting like hell.

The ground was not only three inches further from the ventilation shaft than he remembered, it was also on a different planet than he remembered, but it was the three inches that had caught him by surprise. The offices of *The Hitchhiker's Guide to the Galaxy* were quite often shifted at very short notice to another planet, for reasons of local climate, local hostility, power bills or tax, but they were always reconstructed exactly the same way, almost to the very molecule. For many of the company's employees, the layout of their offices represented the only constant they knew in a severely distorted personal universe.

Something, though, was odd.

This was not in itself surprising, thought Ford as he pulled out his lightweight throwing towel. Virtually everything in his life was, to a greater or lesser extent, odd. It was just that this was odd in a slightly different way than he was used to things being odd, which was, well, strange. He couldn't quite get it into focus immediately.

He got out his No. 3 gauge prising tool.

The alarms were going in the same old way that he knew well. There was a kind of music to them that he could almost hum along to. That was all very familiar. The world outside had been a new one on Ford. He had not been to Saquo-Pilia Hensha before, and he had liked it. It had a kind of carnival atmosphere to it.

He took from his satchel a toy bow and arrow which he had bought in a street market.

He had discovered that the reason for the carnival atmosphere on Saquo-Pilia Hensha was that the local people were celebrating the annual feast of the Assumption of St Antwelm. St Antwelm had been, during his lifetime, a great and popular king who had made a great and popular assumption. What King Antwelm had assumed was that what everybody wanted, all other things being equal, was to be happy and enjoy themselves and have the best possible time together. On his death he had willed his entire personal fortune to financing an annual festival to remind everyone of this, with lots of good food and dancing and very silly games like Hunt the Wocket. His assumption had been such a brilliantly good one that he was made into a saint for it. Not only that, but all the people who had previously been made saints for doing things like being stoned to death in a thoroughly miserable way or living upside down in barrels of dung were instantly demoted and were now thought to be rather embarrassing.

The familiar H-shaped building of the *Hitchhiker's Guide* offices rose above the outskirts of the city, and Ford Prefect had broken into it in the familiar way. He always entered via the ventilation system rather than the main lobby because the main lobby was patrolled by robots whose job it was to quiz incoming employees about their expense accounts. Ford Prefect's expense accounts were notoriously complex and difficult affairs and he had found, on the whole, that the lobby robots were ill-equipped to understand the arguments he wished to put forward in relation to them. He preferred, therefore, to make his entrance by another route.

This meant setting off nearly every alarm in the building, but not the one in the accounts department, which was the way that Ford preferred it.

He hunkered down behind the storage cabinet, he licked the rubber suction cup of the toy arrow, and then fitted it to the string of the bow.

Within about thirty seconds a security robot the size of a small melon came flying down the corridor at about waist height, scanning left and right for anything unusual as it did so.

With impeccable timing Ford shot the toy arrow across its path. The arrow flew across the corridor and stuck, wobbling, on the opposite wall. As it flew, the robot's sensors locked on to it instantly and the robot twisted through ninety degrees to follow it, see what the hell it was and where it was going.

This bought Ford one precious second, during which the robot was looking in the opposite direction from him. He hurled the towel over the flying robot and caught it.

Because of the various sensory protuberances with which the robot was festooned, it couldn't manoeuvre inside the towel, and it just twitched back and forth without being able to turn and face its captor.

Ford hauled it quickly towards him and pinned it down to the ground. It was beginning to whine pitifully. With one swift and practised movement, Ford reached under the towel with his No. 3 gauge prising tool and flipped off the small plastic panel on top of the robot which gave access to its logic circuits.

Now logic is a wonderful thing but it has, as the processes of evolution discovered, certain drawbacks.

Anything that thinks logically can be fooled by something else which thinks at least as logically as it does. The easiest way to fool a completely logical robot is to feed it the same stimulus sequence over and over again so it gets locked in a loop. This was best demonstrated by the famous Herring Sandwich experiments conducted millennia ago at MISPWOSO (The Maximegalon Institute of Slowly and Painfully Working Out the Surprisingly Obvious).

A robot was programmed to believe that it liked herring sandwiches. This was actually the most difficult part of the whole experiment. Once the robot had been programmed to believe that it liked herring sandwiches, a herring sandwich was placed in front of it. Whereupon the robot thought to itself, 'Ah! A herring sandwich! I like herring sandwiches.'

It would then bend over and scoop up the herring sandwich in its herring sandwich scoop, and then straighten up again. Unfortunately for the robot, it was fashioned in such a way that the action of straightening up caused the herring sandwich to slip straight back off its herring sandwich scoop and fall on to the floor in front of the robot. Whereupon the robot thought to itself, 'Ah! A herring sandwich . . .' etc., and repeated the same action over and over and over again. The only thing that prevented the herring sandwich from getting bored with the whole damn business and crawling off in search of other ways of passing the time was that the herring sandwich, being just a bit of dead fish between a couple of slices of bread, was marginally less alert to what was going on than was the robot.

The scientists at the Institute thus discovered the driving force behind all change, development and innovation in life, which was this: herring sandwiches. They published a paper to this effect, which was widely criticized as being extremely stupid. They checked their figures and realized that what they had actually discovered was 'boredom', or rather, the practical function of boredom. In a fever of excitement they then went on to discover other emotions, like 'irritability', 'depression', 'reluctance', 'ickiness' and so on. The next big breakthrough came when they stopped using herring sandwiches, whereupon a whole welter of new emotions became suddenly available to them for study, such as 'relief', 'joy', 'friskiness', 'appetite', 'satisfaction', and most important of all, the desire for 'happiness'.

This was the biggest breakthrough of all.

Vast wodges of complex computer code governing robot behaviour in all possible contingencies could be replaced very simply. All that robots needed was the capacity to be either bored or happy, and a few conditions that needed to be satisfied in order to bring those states about. They would then work the rest out for themselves.

The robot which Ford had got trapped under his towel was not, at the moment, a happy robot. It was happy when it could move about. It was happy when it could see other things. It was particularly happy when it could see other things moving about, particularly if the other things were moving about doing things they shouldn't do because it could then, with considerable delight, report them.

Ford would soon fix that.

He squatted over the robot and held it between his knees. The towel was still covering all of its sensory mechanisms, but Ford had now got its logic circuits exposed. The robot was whirring grungily and pettishly, but it could only fidget, it couldn't actually move. Using the prising tool, Ford eased a small chip out from its socket. As soon as it came out, the robot went quiet and just sat there in a coma.

The chip Ford had taken out was the one which contained the instructions for all the conditions that had to be fulfilled in order for the robot to feel happy. The robot would be happy when a tiny electrical charge from a point just to the left of the chip reached another point just to the right of the chip. The chip determined whether the charge got there or not.

Ford pulled out a small length of wire that had been threaded into the towel. He dug one end of it into the top left hole of the chip socket and the other into the bottom right hole.

That was all it took. Now the robot would be happy whatever happened.

Ford quickly stood up and whisked the towel away. The robot rose ecstatically into the air, pursuing a kind of wriggly path.

It turned and saw Ford.

'Mr Prefect, sir! I'm so happy to see you!'

'Good to see you, little fella,' said Ford.

The robot rapidly reported back to its central control that everything was now for the best in this best of all possible worlds, the alarms rapidly quelled themselves, and life returned to normal.

At least, almost to normal.

There was something odd about the place.

The little robot was gurgling with electric delight. Ford hurried on down the corridor, letting the thing bob along in his wake telling him how delicious everything was, and how happy it was to be able to tell him that.

Ford, however, was not happy.

He passed faces of people he didn't know. They didn't look like his sort of people. They were too well groomed. Their eyes were too dead. Every time he thought he saw someone he recognized in the distance, and hurried along to say hello, it would turn out to be someone else, with an altogether neater hairstyle and a much more thrusting, purposeful look than, well, than anybody Ford knew.

A staircase had been moved a few inches to the left. A ceiling had been lowered slightly. A lobby had been remodelled. All these things were not worrying in themselves, though they were a little disorienting. The thing that was worrying was the decor. It used to be brash and glitzy. Expensive – because the *Guide* sold so well through the civilized and post-civilized Galaxy – but expensive and fun. Wild games machines lined the corridors. Insanely painted grand pianos hung from ceilings, vicious sea creatures from the planet Viv reared up out of pools in tree-filled atria, robot butlers in stupid shirts roamed the corridors seeking whose hands they might press frothing drinks into. People used to have pet vastdragons on leads and pterospondes on perches in their offices. People knew how to have a good time, and if they didn't there were courses they could sign up for which would put that right.

There was none of that now.

Somebody had been through the place doing some iniquitous kind of taste job on it.

Ford turned sharply into a small alcove, cupped his hand and yanked the flying robot in with him. He squatted down and peered at the burbling cybernaut.

'What's been happening here?' he demanded.

'Oh, just the nicest things, sir, just the nicest possible things. Can I sit on your lap, please?'

'No,' said Ford, brushing the thing away. It was overjoyed to be spurned in this way and started to bob and burble and swoon. Ford grabbed it again and stuck it firmly in the air a foot in front of his face. It tried to stay where it was put but couldn't help quivering slightly.

'Something's changed, hasn't it?' Ford hissed.

'Oh yes,' squealed the little robot, 'in the most fabulous and wonderful way. I feel so good about it.'

'Well, what was it like before, then?'

'Scrumptious.'

'But you like the way it's changed?' demanded Ford.

'I like *everything*,' moaned the robot. 'Especially when you shout at me like that. Do it again, *please*.'

'Just tell me what's happened!'

'Oh thank you, thank you!'

Ford sighed.

'OK, OK,' panted the robot. 'The *Guide* has been taken over. There's a new management. It's all so gorgeous I could just melt. The old management was also fabulous, of course, though I'm not sure if I thought so at the time.'

'That was before you had a bit of wire stuck in your head.'

'How true. How wonderfully true. How wonderfully, bubblingly, frothingly, burstingly true. What a truly ecstasy-inducingly correct observation.'

'What's *happened*?' insisted Ford. 'Who is this new management? When did they take over? I . . . oh, never mind,' he added, as the little robot started to gibber with uncontrollable joy and rub itself against his knee. 'I'll go and find out for myself.'

Ford hurled himself at the door of the editor-in-chief's office, tucked himself into a tight ball as the frame splintered and gave way, rolled rapidly across the floor to where the drinks trolley laden with some of the Galaxy's most potent and expensive beverages habitually stood, seized hold of the trolley and, using it to give himself cover, trundled it and himself across the main exposed part of the office floor to where the valuable and extremely rude statue of Leda and the Octopus stood, and took shelter behind it. Meanwhile the little security robot, entering at chest height, was suicidally delighted to draw gunfire away from Ford.

That, at least, was the plan, and a necessary one. The current editor-in-chief, Stagyar-zil-Doggo, was a dangerously unbalanced man who took a homicidal view of contributing staff turning up in his office without pages of fresh, proofed copy, and had a battery of laser-guided guns linked to special scanning devices in the door frame to deter anybody who was merely bringing extremely good reasons why they hadn't written any. Thus was a high level of output maintained.

Unfortunately the drinks trolley wasn't there.

Ford hurled himself desperately sideways and somersaulted towards the statue of Leda and the Octopus, which also wasn't there. He rolled and hurtled around the room in a kind of random panic, tripped, span, hit the window, which fortunately was built to withstand rocket attacks, rebounded, and fell in a bruised and winded heap behind a smart grey crushed-leather sofa, which hadn't been there before.

After a few seconds he slowly peeked up above the top of the sofa. As well as there being no drinks trolley and no Leda and the Octopus, there had also been a startling absence of gunfire. He frowned. This was all utterly wrong.

'Mr Prefect, I assume,' said a voice.

The voice came from a smooth-faced individual behind a large ceramo-teak-bonded desk. Stagyar-zil-Doggo may well have been a hell of an individual, but no one, for a whole variety of reasons, would ever have called him smooth-faced. This was not Stagyar-zil-Doggo.

'I assume from the manner of your entrance that you do not have new material for the, er, *Guide*, at the moment,' said the smooth-faced individual. He was sitting with his elbows resting on the table and holding his fingertips together in a manner which, inexplicably, has never been made a capital offence.

'I've been busy,' said Ford, rather weakly. He staggered to his feet, brushing himself down. Then he thought, what the hell was he saying things weakly for? He had to get on top of this situation. He had to find out who the hell this person was, and he suddenly thought of a way of doing it.

'Who the hell are you?' he demanded.

'I am your new editor-in-chief. That is, if we decide to retain your services. My name is Vann Harl.' He didn't put his hand out. He just added, 'What have you done to that security robot?'

The little robot was rolling very, very slowly round the ceiling and moaning quietly to itself.

'I've made it very happy,' snapped Ford. 'It's a kind of mission I have. Where's Stagyar? More to the point, where's his drinks trolley?'

'Mr zil-Doggo is no longer with this organization. His drinks trolley is, I imagine, helping to console him for this fact.'

'Organization?' yelled Ford. '*Organization?* What a bloody stupid word for a set-up like this!'

'Precisely our sentiments. Under-structured, over-resourced, under-managed, over-inebriated. And that,' said Harl, 'was just the editor.'

'I'll do the jokes,' snarled Ford.

'No,' said Harl. 'You will do the restaurant column.'

He tossed a piece of plastic on to the desk in front of him. Ford did not move to pick it up.

'You *what*?' said Ford.

'No. Me Harl. You Prefect. You do restaurant column. Me editor. Me sit here tell you you do restaurant column. You get?'

'*Restaurant* column?' said Ford, too bewildered to be really angry yet.

'Siddown, Prefect,' said Harl. He swung round in his swivel chair, got to his feet, and stood staring out at the tiny specks enjoying the carnival twenty-three storeys below.

'Time to get this business on its feet, Prefect,' he snapped. 'We at InfiniDim Enterprises are—'

'You at *what*?'

'InfiniDim Enterprises. We have bought out the *Guide*.'

'*Infinidim?*'

'We spent millions on that name, Prefect. Start liking it or start packing.'

Ford shrugged. He had nothing to pack.

'The Galaxy is changing,' said Harl. 'We've got to change with it. Go with the market. The market is moving up. New aspirations. New technology. The future is . . .'

'Don't tell me about the future,' said Ford. 'I've been all over the future. Spend half my time there. It's the same as anywhere else. Anywhen else. Whatever. Just the same old stuff in faster cars and smellier air.'

'That's *one* future,' said Harl. 'That's *your* future, if you accept it. You've got to learn to think multi-dimensionally. There are limitless futures stretching out in every direction from this moment – and from this moment and from this. Billions of them, bifurcating every instant! Every possible position of every possible electron balloons out into billions of probabilities! Billions and billions of shining, gleaming futures! You know what that means?'

'You're dribbling down your chin.'

'Billions and billions of markets!'

'I see,' said Ford. 'So you sell billions and billions of *Guides*.'

'No,' said Harl, reaching for his handkerchief and not finding one. 'Excuse me,' he said, 'but this gets me so excited.' Ford handed him his towel.

'The reason we don't sell billions and billions of *Guides*,' continued Harl, after wiping his mouth, 'is the expense. What we do is we sell one *Guide* billions and billions of times. We exploit the multidimensional nature of the Universe to cut down on manufacturing costs. And we don't sell to penniless hitchhikers. What a stupid notion that was! Find the one section of the market that, more or less by definition, doesn't have any money, and try and sell to it. No. We sell to the affluent business traveller and his vacationing wife in a billion, billion different futures. This is the most radical, dynamic and thrusting business venture in the entire multidimensional infinity of space/time/probability ever.'

'And you want me to be its restaurant critic,' said Ford.

'We would value your input.'

'Kill!' shouted Ford. He shouted it at his towel.

The towel leapt up out of Harl's hands.

This was not because it had any motive force of its own, but because Harl was so startled at the idea that it might. The next thing that startled him was the sight of Ford Prefect hurtling across the desk at him fists first. In fact Ford was just lunging for the credit card, but you don't get to occupy the sort of position that Harl occupied in the sort of organization in which Harl occupied it without developing a healthily paranoid view of life. He took the sensible precaution of hurling himself backwards, and striking his head a sharp blow on the rocket-proof glass, then subsided into a series of worrying and highly personal dreams.

Ford lay on the desk, surprised at how swimmingly everything had gone. He glanced quickly at the piece of plastic he now held in his hand – it was a Dine-O-Charge credit card with his name already embossed on it, and an expiry date two years from now, and was possibly the single most exciting thing Ford had ever seen in his life – then he clambered over the desk to see to Harl.

He was breathing fairly easily. It occurred to Ford that he might breathe more easily yet without the weight of his wallet bearing down on his chest, so he slipped it out of Harl's breast pocket and flipped through it. Fair amount of cash. Credit tokens. Ultragolf club membership. Other club memberships. Photos of someone's wife and family – presumably Harl's, but it was hard to be sure these days. Busy executives often didn't have time for a full-time wife and family and would just rent them for weekends.

Ha!

He couldn't believe what he'd just found.

He slowly drew out from the wallet a single and insanely exciting piece of plastic that was nestling amongst a bunch of receipts.

It wasn't insanely exciting to look at. It was rather dull in fact. It was smaller and a little thicker than a credit card and semi-transparent. If you held it up to the light you could see a lot of holographically encoded information and images buried pseudo-inches deep beneath its surface.

It was an Ident-i-Eeze, and was a very naughty and silly thing for Harl to have lying around in his wallet, though it was perfectly understandable. There were so many different ways in which you were required to provide absolute proof of your identity these days that life could easily become extremely tiresome just from that factor alone, never mind the deeper existential problems of trying to function as a coherent consciousness in an epistemologically ambiguous physical universe. Just look at cash point machines, for instance. Queues of people standing around waiting to have their fingerprints read, their retinas scanned, bits of skin scraped from the nape of the neck and undergoing instant (or nearly instant – a good six or seven seconds in tedious reality) genetic analysis, then having to answer trick questions about members of their family they didn't even remember they had, and about their recorded preferences for tablecloth colours. And that was just to get a bit of spare cash for the weekend. If you were trying to raise a loan for a jetcar, sign a missile treaty or pay an entire restaurant bill things could get really trying.

Hence the Ident-i-Eeze. This encoded every single piece of information about you, your body and your life into one all-purpose machine-readable card that you could then carry around in your wallet, and therefore represented technology's greatest triumph to date over both itself and plain common sense.

Ford pocketed it. A remarkably good idea had just occurred to him. He wondered how long Harl would remain unconscious.

'Hey!' he shouted to the little melon-sized robot still slobbering with euphoria up on the ceiling. 'You want to stay happy?'

The robot gurgled that it did.

'Then stick with me and do everything I tell you without fail.'

The robot said that it was quite happy where it was up on the ceiling thank you very much. It had never realized before how much sheer titillation there was to be got from a good ceiling and it wanted to explore its feelings about ceilings in greater depth.

'You stay there,' said Ford, 'and you'll soon be recaptured and have your conditional chip replaced. You want to stay happy, come now.'

The robot let out a long heartfelt sigh of impassioned tristesse and sank reluctantly away from the ceiling.

'Listen,' said Ford, 'can you keep the rest of the security system happy for a few minutes?'

'One of the joys of true happiness,' trilled the robot, 'is sharing. I brim, I froth, I overflow with . . .'

'OK,' said Ford. 'Just spread a little happiness around the security network. Don't give it any information. Just make it feel good so it doesn't feel the need to ask for any.'

He picked up his towel and ran cheerfully for the door. Life had been a little dull of late. It showed every sign now of becoming extremely froody.

7

Arthur Dent had been in some hell-holes in his life, but he had never before seen a spaceport which had a sign saying, 'Even travelling despondently is better than arriving here.' To welcome visitors the arrivals hall featured a picture of the President of NowWhat, smiling. It was the only picture anybody could find of him, and it had been taken shortly after he had shot himself so although the photo had been retouched as well as could be managed the smile it wore was rather a ghastly one. The side of his head had been drawn back in in crayon. No replacement had been found for the photograph because no replacement had been found for the

President. There was only one ambition which anyone on the planet ever had, and that was to leave.

Arthur checked himself into a small motel on the outskirts of town, and sat glumly on the bed, which was damp, and flipped through the little information brochure, which was also damp. It said that the planet of NowWhat had been named after the opening words of the first settlers to arrive there after struggling across light-years of space to reach the furthest unexplored outreaches of the Galaxy. The main town was called OhWell. There weren't any other towns to speak of. Settlement on NowWhat had not been a success and the sort of people who actually wanted to live on NowWhat were not the sort of people you would want to spend time with.

Trading was mentioned in the brochure. The main trade that was carried out was in the skins of the NowWhattian boghog but it wasn't a very successful one because no one in their right minds would want to buy a NowWhattian boghog skin. The trade only hung on by its fingernails because there was always a significant number of people in the Galaxy who were not in their right minds. Arthur had felt very uncomfortable looking around at some of the other occupants of the small passenger compartment of the ship.

The brochure described some of the history of the planet. Whoever had written it had obviously started out trying to drum up a little enthusiasm for the place by stressing that it wasn't actually cold and wet *all* the time, but could find little positive to add to this so the tone of the piece quickly degenerated into savage irony.

It talked about the early years of settlement. It said that the major activities pursued on NowWhat were those of catching, skinning and eating NowWhattian boghogs, which were the only extant form of animal life on NowWhat, all other having long ago died of despair.

The boghogs were tiny, vicious creatures, and the small margin by which they fell short of being completely inedible was the margin by which life on the planet subsisted. So what were the rewards, however small, that made life on NowWhat worth living? Well, there weren't any. Not a one. Even making yourself some protective clothing out of boghog skins was an exercise in disappointment and futility, since the skins were unaccountably thin and leaky. This caused a lot of puzzled conjecture amongst the settlers. What was the boghog's secret of keeping warm? If anyone had ever learnt the language the boghogs spoke to each other they would have discovered that there was no trick. The boghogs were as cold and wet as anyone else on the planet. No one had had the slightest desire to learn the language of the boghogs for the simple reason that these creatures communicated by biting each other very hard on the thigh. Life on NowWhat being what it was, most of what a boghog might have to say about it could easily be signified by these means.

Arthur flipped through the brochure till he found what he was looking for. At the back there were a few maps of the planet. They were fairly rough and ready because they weren't likely to be of much interest to anyone, but they told him what he wanted to know.

He didn't recognize it at first because the maps were the other way up from the way he would have expected and looked, therefore, thoroughly unfamiliar. Of course, up and down, north and south, are absolutely arbitrary designations, but we are used to seeing things the way we are used to seeing them, and Arthur had to turn the maps upside-down to make sense of them.

There was one huge landmass off on the upper left-hand side of the page which tapered down to a tiny waist and then ballooned out again like a large comma. On the right-hand side was a collection of large shapes jumbled familiarly together. The outlines were not exactly the same, and Arthur didn't know if this was because the map was so rough, or because the sea-level was higher or because, well, things were just different here. But the evidence was inarguable.

This was definitely the Earth.

Or rather, it most definitely was not.

It merely looked a lot like the Earth and occupied the same co-ordinates in space–time. What co-ordinates it occupied in probability was anybody's guess.

He sighed.

This, he realized, was about as close to home as he was likely to get. Which meant that he was about as far from home as he could possibly be. Glumly he slapped the brochure shut and wondered what on earth he was going to do next.

He allowed himself a hollow laugh at what he had just thought. He looked at his old watch, and shook it a bit to wind it. It had taken him, according to his own timescale, a year of hard travelling to get here. A year since the accident in hyperspace in which Fenchurch had completely vanished. One minute she had been sitting there next to him in the SlumpJet; the next minute the ship had done a perfectly normal hyperspace hop and when he had next looked she was not there. The seat wasn't even warm. Her name wasn't even on the passenger list.

The spaceline had been wary of him when he had complained. A lot of awkward things happen in space travel, and a lot of them make a lot of money for lawyers. But when they had asked him what Galactic Sector he and Fenchurch had been from and he had said ZZ9 Plural Z Alpha they had relaxed completely in a way that Arthur wasn't at all sure he liked. They even laughed a little, though sympathetically, of course. They pointed to the clause in the ticket contract which said that the entities whose lifespans had originated in any of the Plural zones were advised not to travel in hyperspace and did so at their own risk. Everybody, they said, knew that. They tittered slightly and shook their heads.

As Arthur had left their offices he found he was trembling slightly. Not only had he lost Fenchurch in the most complete and utter way possible, but he felt that the more time he spent away out in the Galaxy the more it seemed that the number of things he didn't know anything about actually increased.

Just as he was lost for a moment in these numb memories a knock came on the door of his motel room, which then opened immediately. A fat and dishevelled man came in carrying Arthur's one small case.

He got as far as, 'Where shall I put—' when there was a sudden violent flurry and he collapsed heavily against the door, trying to beat off a small and mangy creature that had leapt snarling out of the wet night and buried its teeth in his thigh, even through the thick layers of leather padding he wore there. There was a brief, ugly confusion of jabbering and thrashing. The man shouted frantically and pointed. Arthur grabbed a hefty stick that stood next to the door expressly for this purpose and beat at the boghog with it.

The boghog suddenly disengaged and limped backwards, dazed and forlorn. It turned anxiously in the corner of the room, its tail tucked up right under its back legs, and stood looking nervously up at Arthur, jerking its head awkwardly and repeatedly to one side. Its jaw seemed to be dislocated. It cried a little and scraped its damp tail across the floor. By the door, the fat man with Arthur's suitcase was sitting and cursing, trying to staunch the flow of blood from his thigh. His clothes were already wet from the rain.

Arthur stared at the boghog, not knowing what to do.

The boghog looked at him questioningly. It tried to approach him, making mournful little whimpering noises. It moved its jaw painfully. It made a sudden leap for Arthur's thigh, but its dislocated jaw was too weak to get a grip and it sank, whining sadly, down to the floor. The fat man jumped to his feet, grabbed the stick, beat the boghog's brains into a sticky, pulpy mess on the thin carpet, and then stood there breathing heavily as if daring the animal to move again, just once.

A single boghog eyeball sat looking reproachfully at Arthur from out of the mashed ruins of its head.

'What do you think it was trying to say?' asked Arthur in a small voice.

'Ah, nothing much,' said the man. 'Just its way of trying to be friendly. This is just our way of being friendly back,' he added, gripping the stick.

'When's the next flight out?' asked Arthur.

'Thought you'd only just arrived,' said the man.

'Yes,' said Arthur. 'It was only going to be a brief visit. I just wanted to see if this was the right place or not. Sorry.'

'You mean you're on the wrong planet?' said the man lugubriously. 'Funny how many people say that. Specially the people who live here.' He eyed the remains of the boghog with a deep, ancestral resentment.

'Oh no,' said Arthur, 'it's the right planet all right.' He picked up the damp brochure lying on the bed and put it in his pocket. 'It's OK, thanks, I'll take that,' he said, taking his case from the man. He went to the door and looked out into the cold, wet night.

'Yes, it's the right planet, all right,' he said again. 'Right planet, wrong universe.'

A single bird wheeled in the sky above him as he set off back for the spaceport.

8

Ford had his own code of ethics. It wasn't much of one, but it was his and he stuck by it, more or less. One rule he made was never to buy his own drinks. He wasn't sure if that counted as an ethic, but you have to go with what you've got. He was also firmly and utterly opposed to all and any forms of cruelty to any animals whatsoever except geese. And furthermore he would never steal from his employers.

Well, not exactly *steal*.

If his accounts supervisor didn't start to hyperventilate and put out a seal-all-exits security alert when Ford handed in his expenses claim then Ford felt he wasn't doing his job properly. But actually *stealing* was another thing. That was biting the hand that feeds you. Sucking very hard on it, even nibbling it in an affectionate kind of a way was OK, but you didn't actually bite it. Not when that hand was the *Guide*. The *Guide* was something sacred and special.

But that, thought Ford as he ducked and weaved his way down through the building, was about to change. And they had only themselves to blame. Look at all this stuff. Lines of neat grey office cubicles and executive workstation pods. The whole place was dreary with the hum of memos and minutes of meetings flitting through its electronic networks. Out in the street they were playing Hunt the Wocket, for Zark's sake, but here in the very heart of the *Guide* offices no one was even recklessly kicking a ball around the corridors or wearing inappropriately coloured beachware.

'InfiniDim Enterprises,' Ford snarled to himself as he stalked rapidly down one corridor after another. Door after door magically opened to him without question.

Elevators took him happily to places they should not. Ford was trying to pursue the most tangled and complicated route he could, heading generally downwards through the building. His happy little robot took care of everything, spreading waves of acquiescent joy through all the security circuits it encountered.

Ford thought it needed a name and decided to call it Emily Saunders, after a girl he had very fond memories of. Then he thought that Emily Saunders was an absurd name for a security robot, and decided to call it Colin instead, after Emily's dog.

He was moving deep into the bowels of the building now, into areas he had never entered before, areas of higher and higher security. He was beginning to encounter puzzled looks from the operatives he passed. At this level of security you didn't even call them people any more. And they were probably doing stuff that only operatives would do. When they went home to their families in the evening they became people again, and when their little children looked up to them with their sweet shining eyes and said 'Daddy, what did you do all day today?' they just said, 'I performed my duties as an operative,' and left it at that.

The truth of the matter was that all sorts of highly dodgy stuff went on behind the cheery, happy-go-lucky front that the *Guide* liked to put up – or used to like to put up before this new InfiniDim Enterprises bunch marched in and started to make the whole thing highly dodgy. There were all kinds of tax scams and rackets and graft and shady deals supporting the shining edifice, and down in the secure research and data-processing levels of the building was where it all went on.

Every few years the *Guide* would set up its business, and indeed its building on a new world, and all would be sunshine and laughter for a while as the *Guide* would put down its roots in the local culture and economy, provide employment, a sense of glamour and adventure and, in the end, not quite as much actual revenue as the locals had expected.

When the *Guide* moved on, taking its building with it, it left a little like a thief in the night. Exactly like a thief in the night, in fact. It usually left in the very early hours of the morning, and the following day there always turned out to be a very great deal of stuff missing. Whole cultures and economies would collapse in its wake, often within a week, leaving once thriving planets desolate and shell-shocked but still somehow feeling they had been part of some great adventure.

The 'operatives' who shot puzzled glances at Ford as he marched on into the depths of the building's most sensitive areas were reassured by the presence of Colin, who was flying along with him in a buzz of emotional fulfilment and easing his path for him at every stage.

Alarms were starting to go off in other parts of the building. Perhaps that meant that Vann Harl had already been discovered, which might be a problem. Ford had been hoping he would be able to slip the Ident-i-Eeze back into his pocket before he came round. Well, that was a problem for later, and he didn't for the moment have the faintest idea how he was going to solve it. For the moment he wasn't going to worry. Wherever he went with little Colin, he was surrounded by a cocoon of sweetness and light and, most importantly, willing and acquiescent elevators and positively obsequious doors.

Ford even began to whistle, which was probably his mistake. Nobody likes a whistler, particularly not the divinity that shapes our ends.

The next door wouldn't open.

And that was a pity, because it was the very one that

Ford had been making for. It stood there before him, grey and resolutely closed with a sign on it saying:

NO ADMITTANCE.
NOT EVEN TO AUTHORIZED PERSONNEL.
YOU ARE WASTING YOUR TIME HERE.
GO AWAY.

Colin reported that the doors had been getting generally a lot grimmer down in these lower reaches of the building.

They were about ten storeys below ground level now. The air was refrigerated and the tasteful grey hessian wall-weave had given way to brutal grey bolted steel walls. Colin's rampant euphoria had subsided into a kind of determined cheeriness. He said that he was beginning to tire a little. It was taking all his energy to pump the slightest bonhomie whatsoever into the doors down here.

Ford kicked at the door. It opened.

'Mixture of pleasure and pain,' he muttered. 'Always does the trick.'

He walked in and Colin flew in after him. Even with a wire stuck straight into his pleasure electrode his happiness was a nervous kind of happiness. He bobbed around a little.

The room was small, grey and humming.

This was the nerve centre of the entire *Guide*.

The computer terminals that lined the grey walls were windows on to every aspect of the *Guide*'s operations. Here, on the left-hand side of the room, reports were gathered over the Sub-Etha Net from field researchers in every corner of the Galaxy, fed straight up into the network of sub-editors' offices where they had all the good bits cut out by secretaries because the sub-editors were out having lunch. The remaining copy would then be shot across to the other half of the building – the other leg of the 'H' – which was the legal department. The legal department would cut out anything that was still even remotely good from what remained and fire it back to the offices of the executive editors, who were also out at lunch. So the editors' secretaries would read it and say it was stupid and cut most of what was left.

When any of the editors finally staggered in from lunch they would exclaim 'What is this feeble crap that X' – where X was the name of the field researcher in question – 'has sent us from half-way across the bloody Galaxy? What's the point of having somebody spending three whole orbital periods out in the bloody Gagrakacka Mind Zones, with all that stuff going on out there, if this load of anaemic squitter is the best he can be bothered to send us. Disallow his expenses!'

'What shall we do with the copy?' the secretary would ask.

'Ah, put it out over the network. Got to have something going out there. I've got a headache, I'm going home.'

So the edited copy would go for one last slash and burn through the legal department, and then be sent back down here where it would be broadcast out over the Sub-Etha Net for instantaneous retrieval anywhere in the Galaxy. That was handled by equipment which was monitored and controlled by the terminals on the right-hand side of the room.

Meanwhile the order to disallow the researcher's expenses was relayed down to the computer terminal stuck off in the right-hand corner, and it was to this terminal that Ford Prefect now swiftly made his way.

(If you are reading this on planet Earth then:

a) Good luck to you. There is an awful lot of stuff you don't know anything about, but you are not alone in this. It's just that in your case the consequences of not knowing any of this stuff are particularly terrible, but then, hey, that's just the way the cookie gets completely stomped on and obliterated.

b) Don't imagine you know what a computer terminal is.

A computer terminal is not some clunky old television with a typewriter in front of it. It is an interface where the mind and body can connect with the universe and move bits of it about.)

Ford hurried over to the terminal, sat in front of it and quickly dipped himself into its universe.

It wasn't the normal universe he knew. It was a universe of densely enfolded worlds, of wild topographies, towering mountain peaks, heart-stopping ravines, of moons shattering off into sea horses, hurtful blurting crevices, silently heaving oceans and bottomless hurtling hooping funts.

He held still to get his bearings. He controlled his breathing, closed his eyes and looked again.

So this was where accountants spent their time. There was clearly more to them than met the eye. He looked around carefully, trying not to let it all swell and swim and overwhelm him.

He didn't know his way around this universe. He didn't even know the physical laws that determined its dimensional extents or behaviours, but his instinct told him to look for the most outstanding feature he could detect and make towards it.

Way off in some indistinguishable distance – was it a mile or a million or a mote in his eye? – was a stunning peak that overarched the sky, climbed and climbed and spread out in flowering aigrettes,[1] agglomerates,[2] and archimandrites.[3]

1 An ornamental tuft of plumes.

2 A jumbled mass.

3 A cleric ranking below a bishop.

He weltered towards it, hooling and thurling, and at last reached it in a meaninglessly long umthingth of time.

He clung to it, arms outspread, gripping tightly on to its roughly gnarled and pitted surface. Once he was certain that he was secure he made the hideous mistake of looking down.

While he had been weltering, hooling and thurling, the distance beneath him had not bothered him unduly, but now that he was gripping, the distance made his heart wilt and his brain bend. His fingers were white with pain and tension. His teeth were grinding and twisting against each other beyond his control. His eyes turned inwards with waves from the willowing extremities of nausea.

With an immense effort of will and faith he simply let go and pushed.

He felt himself float. Away. And then, counter-intuitively, upwards. And upwards.

He threw his shoulders back, let his arms drop, gazed upwards and let himself be drawn loosely, higher and higher.

Before long, insofar as such terms had any meaning in this virtual universe, a ledge loomed up ahead of him on which he could grip and on to which he could clamber.

He rose, he gripped, he clambered.

He panted a little. This was all a little stressful.

He held tightly on to the ledge as he sat. He wasn't certain if this was to prevent himself from falling down off it or rising up from it, but he needed something to grip on to as he surveyed the world in which he found himself.

The whirling, turning height span him and twisted his brain in upon itself till he found himself, eyes closed, whimpering and hugging the hideous wall of towering rock.

He slowly brought his breathing back under control again. He told himself repeatedly that he was just in a graphic representation of a world. A virtual universe. A simulated reality. He could snap back out of it at any moment.

He snapped back out of it.

He was sitting in a blue leatherette foam-filled swivel-seated office chair in front of a computer terminal.

He relaxed.

He was clinging to the face of an impossibly high peak perched on a narrow ledge above a drop of brain-swivelling dimensions.

It wasn't just the landscape being so far beneath him – he wished it would stop undulating and waving.

He had to get a grip. Not on the rock wall – that was an illusion. He had to get a grip on the situation, be able to look at the physical world he was in while drawing himself out of it emotionally.

He clenched inwardly and then, just as he had let go of the rock face itself, he let go of the idea of the rock face and let himself just sit there clearly and freely. He looked out at the world. He was breathing well. He was cool. He was in charge again.

He was in a four-dimensional topological model of the *Guide*'s financial systems, and somebody or something would very shortly want to know why.

And here they came.

Swooping through virtual space towards him came a small flock of mean and steely-eyed creatures with pointy little heads, pencil moustaches and querulous demands as to who he was, what he was doing there, what his authorization was, what the authorization of his authorizing agent was, what his inside leg measurement was and so on. Laser light flickered all over him as if he was a packet of biscuits at a supermarket check-out. The heavier duty laser guns were held, for the moment, in reserve. The fact that all of this was happening in virtual space made no difference. Being virtually killed by a virtual laser in virtual space is just as effective as the real thing, because you are as dead as you think you are.

The laser readers were becoming very agitated as they flickered over his fingerprints, his retina and the follicle pattern where his hair line was receding. They didn't like what they were finding at all. The chattering and screeching of highly personal and insolent questions was rising in pitch. A little surgical steel scraper was reaching out towards the skin at the nape of his neck when Ford, holding his breath and praying very slightly, pulled Vann Harl's Ident-i-Eeze out of his pocket and waved it in front of them.

Instantly every laser was diverted to the little card and swept backwards and forwards over it and in it, examining and reading every molecule.

Then, just as suddenly, they stopped.

The entire flock of little virtual inspectors snapped to attention.

'Nice to see you, Mr Harl,' they said in smarmy unison. 'Is there anything we can do for you?'

Ford smiled a slow and vicious smile.

'Do you know,' he said, 'I rather think there is.'

Five minutes later he was out of there.

About thirty seconds to do the job, and three minutes thirty to cover his tracks. He could have done anything he liked in the virtual structure, more or less. He could have transferred ownership of the entire organization into his own name, but he doubted if that would have gone unnoticed. He didn't want it anyway. It would have meant responsibility, working late nights at the office, not to mention massive and time-consuming fraud investigations and a fair amount of time in jail. He wanted something that nobody other than the computer would notice: that was the bit that took thirty seconds.

The thing that took three minutes thirty was programming the computer not to notice that it had noticed anything.

It had to *want* not to know about what Ford was up to, and then he could safely leave the computer to rationalize its own defences against the information ever emerging. It was a programming technique that had been reverse-engineered from the sort of psychotic mental blocks that otherwise perfectly normal people had been observed invariably to develop when elected to high political office.

The other minute was spent discovering that the computer system already had a mental block. A big one.

He would never have discovered it if he hadn't been busy engineering a mental block himself. He came across a whole slew of smooth and plausible denial procedures and diversionary subroutines exactly where he had been planning to install his own. The computer denied all knowledge of them, of course, then blankly refused to accept that there was anything even to deny knowledge of, and was generally so convincing that even Ford almost found himself thinking he must have made a mistake.

He was impressed.

He was so impressed, in fact, that he didn't bother to install his own mental block procedures, he just set up calls to the ones that were already there, which then called themselves when questioned, and so on.

He quickly set about debugging the little bits of code he had installed himself, only to discover they weren't there. Cursing, he searched all over for them, but could find no trace of them at all.

He was just about to start installing them all over again when he realized that the reason he couldn't find them was that they were working already.

He grinned with satisfaction.

He tried to discover what the computer's other mental block was all about, but it seemed, not unnaturally, to have a mental block about it. He could no longer find any trace of it at all, in fact; it was that good. He wondered if he had been imagining it. He wondered if he had been imagining that it was something to do with something in the building, and something to do with the number 13. He ran a few tests. Yes, he had obviously been imagining it.

No time for fancy routes now, there was obviously a major security alert in progress. Ford took the elevator up to the ground floor to change to the express elevators. He had somehow to get the Ident-i-Eeze back into Harl's pocket before it was missed. How, he didn't know.

The doors of the elevator slid open to reveal a large posse of security guards and robots poised waiting for it and brandishing filthy looking weapons.

They ordered him out.

With a shrug he stepped forward. They all pushed rudely past him. into the elevator which took them down to continue their search for him on the lower levels.

This was fun, thought Ford, giving Colin a friendly pat. Colin was about the first genuinely useful robot Ford had ever encountered. Colin bobbed along in the air in front of him in a lather of cheerful ecstasy. Ford was glad he'd named him after a dog.

He was highly tempted just to leave at that point and

hope for the best, but he knew that the best had a far greater chance of actually occurring if Harl did not discover that his Ident-i-Eeze was missing. He had somehow, surreptitiously, to return it.

They went to the express elevators.

'Hi,' said the elevator they got into.

'Hi,' said Ford.

'Where can I take you folks today?' said the elevator.

'Floor 23,' said Ford.

'Seems to be a popular floor today,' said the elevator.

'Hmm,' thought Ford, not liking the sound of that at all. The elevator lit up the twenty-third floor on its floor display and started to zoom upwards. Something about the floor display tweaked at Ford's mind but he couldn't catch what it was and forgot about it. He was more worried about the idea of the floor he was going to being a popular one. He hadn't really thought through how he was going to deal with whatever it was that was happening up there because he had no idea what he was going to find. He would just have to busk it.

They were there.

The doors slid open.

Ominous quiet.

Empty corridor.

There was the door to Harl's office, with a slight layer of dust around it. Ford knew that this dust consisted of billions of tiny molecular robots that had crawled out of the woodwork, built each other, rebuilt the door, disassembled each other and then crept back into the woodwork again and just waited for damage. Ford wondered what kind of life that was, but not for long because he was a lot more concerned about what his own life was like at that moment.

He took a deep breath and started his run.

9

Arthur felt at a bit of a loss. There was a whole Galaxy of stuff out there for him, and he wondered if it was churlish of him to complain to himself that it lacked just two things: the world he was born on and the woman he loved.

Damn it and blast it, he thought, and felt the need of some guidance and advice. He consulted *The Hitchhiker's Guide to the Galaxy*. He looked up 'guidance' and it said 'See under ADVICE'. He looked up 'advice' and it said 'See under GUIDANCE'. It had been doing a lot of that kind of stuff recently and he wondered if it was all it was cracked up to be.

He headed to the outer Eastern Rim of the Galaxy where, it was said, wisdom and truth were to be found, most particularly on the planet Hawalius, which was a planet of oracles and seers and soothsayers and also take-away pizza shops, because most mystics were completely incapable of cooking for themselves.

However it appeared that some sort of calamity had befallen this planet. As Arthur wandered the streets of the village where the major prophets lived, it had something of a crestfallen air. He came across one prophet who was clearly shutting up shop in a despondent kind of way and asked him what was happening.

'No call for us any more,' he said gruffly as he started to bang a nail into the plank he was holding across the window of his hovel.

'Oh? Why's that?'

'Hold on to the other end of this and I'll show you.'

Arthur held up the unnailed end of the plank and the old prophet scuttled into the recesses of his hovel, returning a moment or two later with a small Sub-Etha radio. He turned it on, fiddled with the dial for a moment and put the thing on the small wooden bench that he usually sat and prophesied on. He then took hold of the plank again and resumed hammering.

Arthur sat and listened to the radio.

'. . . be confirmed,' said the radio.

'Tomorrow,' it continued, 'the Vice-President of Poffla Vigus, Roopy Ga Stip, will announce that he intends to run for President. In a speech he will give tomorrow at . . .'

'Find another channel,' said the prophet. Arthur pushed the preset button.

'. . . refused to comment,' said the radio. 'Next week's jobless totals in the Zabush sector,' it continued, 'will be the worst since records began. A report published next month says . . .'

'Find another,' barked the prophet, crossly. Arthur pushed the button again.

'. . . denied it categorically,' said the radio. 'Next month's Royal Wedding between Prince Gid of the Soofling Dynasty and Princess Hooli of Raui Alpha will be the most spectacular ceremony the Bjanjy Territories has ever witnessed. Our reporter Trillian Astra is there and sends us this report.'

Arthur blinked.

The sound of cheering crowds and a hubbub of brass bands erupted from the radio. A very familiar voice said, 'Well, Krart, the scene here in the middle of next month is absolutely incredible. Princess Hooli is looking radiant in a . . .'

The prophet swiped the radio off the bench and on to the dusty ground, where it squawked like a badly tuned chicken.

'See what we have to contend with?' grumbled the prophet. 'Here, hold this. Not that, this. No, not like that. This way up. Other way round, you fool.'

'I was listening to that,' complained Arthur, grappling helplessly with the prophet's hammer.

'So does everybody. That's why this place is like a ghost town.' He spat into the dust.

'No, I mean, that sounded like someone I knew.'

'Princess Hooli? If I had to stand around saying hello to everybody who's known Princess Hooli I'd need a new set of lungs.'

'Not the Princess,' said Arthur. 'The reporter. Her name's Trillian. I don't know where she got the Astra from. She's from the same planet as me. I wondered where she'd got to.'

'Oh, she's all over the continuum these days. We can't get the tri-D TV stations out here of course, thank the Great Green Arkleseizure, but you hear her on the radio, gallivanting here and there through space-time. She wants to settle down and find herself a steady era, that young lady does. It'll all end in tears. Probably already has.' He swung with his hammer and hit his thumb rather hard. He started to speak in tongues.

The village of oracles wasn't much better.

He had been told that when looking for a good oracle it was best to find the oracle that other oracles went to, but he was shut. There was a sign by the entrance saying, 'I just don't know any more. Try next door, but that's just a suggestion, not formal oracular advice.'

'Next door' was a cave a few hundred yards away and Arthur walked towards it. Smoke and steam were rising from, respectively, a small fire and a battered tin pot that was hanging over it. There was also a very nasty smell coming from the pot. At least, Arthur thought it was coming from the pot. The distended bladders of some of the local goat-like things were hanging from a propped-up line drying in the sun, and the smell could have been coming from them. There was also, a worryingly small distance away, a pile of discarded bodies of the local goat-like things and the smell could have been coming from them.

But the smell could just as easily have been coming from the old lady who was busy beating flies away from the pile of bodies. It was a hopeless task because each of the flies was about the size of a winged bottle top and all she had was a table tennis bat. Also she seemed half blind. Every now and then, by chance, her wild thrashing would connect with one of the flies with a richly satisfying thunk, and the fly would hurtle through the air and smack itself open against the rock face a few yards from the entrance to her cave.

She gave every impression, by her demeanour, that these were the moments she lived for.

Arthur watched this exotic performance for a while from a polite distance, and then at last tried giving a gentle cough to attract her attention. The gentle cough, courteously meant, unfortunately involved first inhaling rather more of the local atmosphere than he had so far been doing and as a result, he erupted into a fit of raucous expectoration, and collapsed against the rock face, choking and streaming with tears. He struggled for breath, but each new breath made things worse. He vomited, half-choked again, rolled over his vomit, kept rolling for a few yards, and eventually made it up on to his hands and knees and crawled, panting, into slightly fresher air.

'Excuse me,' he said. He got some breath back. 'I really am most dreadfully sorry. I feel a complete idiot and . . .' He gestured helplessly towards the small pile of his own vomit lying spread around the entrance to her cave.

'What can I say?' he said. 'What can I possibly say?'

This at least had gained her attention. She looked round at him suspiciously, but, being half blind, had difficulty finding him in the blurred and rocky landscape.

He waved, helpfully. 'Hello!' he called.

At last she spotted him, grunted to herself and turned back to whacking flies.

It was horribly apparent from the way that currents of air moved when she did that the major source of the smell was in fact her. The drying bladders, the festering bodies and the noxious potage may all have been making violent contributions to the atmosphere, but the major olfactory presence was the woman herself.

She got another good thwack at a fly. It smacked against the rock and dribbled its insides down it in what she clearly regarded, if she could see that far, as a satisfactory manner.

Unsteadily, Arthur got to his feet and brushed himself down with a fistful of dried grass. He didn't know what else to do by way of announcing himself. He had half a mind just to wander off again, but felt awkward about leaving a pile of his vomit in front of the entrance to the woman's home. He wondered what to do about it. He started to pluck up more handfuls of the scrubby dried grass that was to be found here and there. He was worried, though, that if he ventured nearer to the vomit he might simply add to it rather than clear it up.

Just as he was debating with himself as to what the right course of action was he began to realize that she was at last saying something to him.

'I beg your pardon?' he called out.

'I said, can I help you?' she said, in a thin, scratchy voice, that he could only just hear.

'Er, I came to ask your advice,' he called back, feeling a bit ridiculous.

She turned to peer at him, myopically, then turned back, swiped at a fly and missed.

'What about?' she said.

'I beg your pardon?' he said.

'I said, what about?' she almost screeched.

'Well,' said Arthur. 'Just sort of general advice, really. It said in the brochure—'

'Ha! Brochure!' spat the old woman. She seemed to be waving her bat more or less at random now.

Arthur fished the crumpled-up brochure from his pocket. He wasn't quite certain why. He had already read it and she, he expected, wouldn't want to. He unfolded it anyway in order to have something to frown thoughtfully at for a moment or two. The copy in the brochure wittered on about the ancient mystical arts of the seers and sages of Hawalius, and wildly over-represented the level of accommodation available in Hawalion. Arthur still carried a copy of *The Hitchhiker's Guide to the Galaxy* with him but found, when he consulted it, that the entries were becoming more abstruse and paranoid and had lots of *x*'s and *j*'s and *{*'s in them. Something was wrong somewhere. Whether it was in his own personal unit, or whether it was something or someone going terribly amiss, or perhaps just hallucinating, at the heart of the *Guide* organization itself, he didn't know. But one way or another he was even less inclined to trust it than usual, which meant that he trusted it not one bit, and mostly used it for eating his sandwiches off when he was sitting on a rock staring at something.

The woman had turned and was walking slowly towards him now. Arthur tried, without making it too obvious, to judge the wind direction, and bobbed about a bit as she approached.

'Advice,' she said. 'Advice, eh?'

'Er, yes,' said Arthur. 'Yes, that is . . .'

He frowned again at the brochure, as if to be certain that he hadn't misread it and stupidly turned up on the wrong planet or something. The brochure said: 'The friendly local inhabitants will be glad to share with you the knowledge and wisdom of the ancients. Peer with them into the swirling mysteries of past and future time!' There were some coupons as well, but Arthur had been far too embarrassed actually to cut them out or try to present them to anybody.

'Advice, eh,' said the old woman again. 'Just sort of general advice, you say. On what? What to do with your life, that sort of thing?'

'Yes,' said Arthur. 'That sort of thing. Bit of a problem I sometimes find, if I'm being perfectly honest.' He was trying desperately, with tiny darting movements, to stay upwind of her. She surprised him by suddenly turning sharply away from him and heading off towards her cave.

'You'll have to help me with the photocopier, then,' she said.

'What?' said Arthur.

'The photocopier,' she repeated, patiently. 'You'll have to help me drag it out. It's solar-powered. I have to keep it in the cave, though, so the birds don't shit on it.'

'I see,' said Arthur.

'I'd take a few deep breaths if I were you,' muttered the old woman, as she stomped into the gloom of the cave mouth.

Arthur did as she advised. He almost hyperventilated in fact. When he felt he was ready, he held his breath and followed her in.

The photocopier was a big old thing on a rickety trolley. It stood just inside the dim shadows of the cave. The wheels were stuck obstinately in different directions and the ground was rough and stony.

'Go ahead and take a breath outside,' said the old woman. Arthur was going red in the face trying to help her move the thing.

He nodded in relief. If she wasn't going to be embarrassed about it then neither, he was determined, would he. He stepped outside and took a few breaths, then came back in to do more heaving and pushing. He had to do this quite a few times till at last the machine was outside.

The sun beat down on it. The old woman disappeared back into her cave again and brought with her some mottled metal panels, which she connected to the machine to collect the sun's energy.

She squinted up into the sky. The sun was quite bright, but the day was hazy and vague.

'It'll take a while,' she said.

Arthur said he was happy to wait.

The old woman shrugged and stomped across to the fire. Above it, the contents of the tin can were bubbling away. She poked about at them with a stick.

'You won't be wanting any lunch?' she enquired of Arthur.

'I've eaten, thanks,' said Arthur. 'No, really. I've eaten.'

'I'm sure you have,' said the old lady. She stirred with the stick. After a few minutes she fished a lump of something out, blew on it to cool it a little, and then put it in her mouth.

She chewed on it thoughtfully for a bit.

Then she hobbled slowly across to the pile of dead goat-like things. She spat the lump out on to the pile. She hobbled slowly back to the can. She tried to unhook it from the sort of tripod-like thing that it was hanging from.

'Can I help you?' said Arthur, jumping up politely. He hurried over.

Together they disengaged the tin from the tripod and carried it awkwardly down the slight slope that led downwards from her cave and towards a line of scrubby and gnarled trees, which marked the edge of a steep but quite shallow gully, from which a whole new range of offensive smells was emanating.

'Ready?' said the old lady.

'Yes . . .' said Arthur, though he didn't know for what.

'One,' said the old lady.

'Two,' she said.

'Three,' she added.

Arthur realized just in time what she intended. Together they tossed the contents of the tin into the gully.

After an hour or two of uncommunicative silence, the old woman decided that the solar panels had absorbed enough sunlight to run the photocopier now and she disappeared to rummage inside her cave. She emerged at last with a few sheaves of paper and fed them through the machine.

She handed the copies to Arthur.

'This is, er, this your advice, then, is it?' said Arthur, leafing through them uncertainly.

'No,' said the old lady. 'It's the story of my life. You see, the quality of any advice anybody has to offer has to be judged against the quality of life they actually lead. Now, as you look through this document you'll see that I've underlined all the major decisions I ever made to make them stand out. They're all indexed and cross-referenced. See? All I can suggest is that if you take decisions that are exactly opposite to the sort of decisions that I've taken, then maybe you won't finish up at the end of your life . . .' she paused, and filled her lungs for a good shout, '. . . in a smelly old cave like this!'

She grabbed up her table tennis bat, rolled up her

sleeves, stomped off to her pile of dead goat-like things, and started to set about the flies with vim and vigour.

The last village Arthur visited consisted entirely of extremely high poles. They were so high that it wasn't possible to tell, from the ground, what was on top of them, and Arthur had to climb three before he found one that had anything on top of it at all other than a platform covered with bird droppings.

Not an easy task. You went up the poles by climbing on the short wooden pegs that had been hammered into them in slowly ascending spirals. Anybody who was a less diligent tourist than Arthur would have taken a couple of snapshots and sloped right off to the nearest Bar & Grill, where you also could buy a range of particularly sweet and gooey chocolate cakes to eat in front of the ascetics. But, largely as a result of this, most of the ascetics had gone now. In fact they had mostly gone and set up lucrative therapy centres on some of the more affluent worlds in the North West Ripple of the Galaxy, where the living was easier by a factor of about seventeen million, and the chocolate was just fabulous. Most of the ascetics, it turned out, had not known about chocolate before they took up asceticism. Most of the clients who came to their therapy centres knew about it all too well.

At the top of the third pole Arthur stopped for a breather. He was very hot and out of breath, since each pole was about fifty or sixty feet high. The world seemed to swing vertiginously around him, but it didn't worry Arthur too much. He knew that, logically, he could not die until he had been to Stavromula Beta,[4] and had therefore managed to cultivate a merry attitude towards extreme personal danger. He felt a little giddy

4 See *Life, the Universe and Everything*, Chapter 18.

perched fifty feet up in the air on top of a pole, but he dealt with it by eating a sandwich. He was just about to embark on reading the photocopied life history of the oracle, when he was rather startled to hear a slight cough behind him.

He turned so abruptly that he dropped his sandwich, which turned downwards through the air and was rather small by the time it was stopped by the ground.

About thirty feet behind Arthur was another pole, and, alone amongst the sparse forest of about three dozen poles, the top of it was occupied. It was occupied by an old man who, in turn, seemed to be occupied by profound thoughts that were making him scowl.

'Excuse me,' said Arthur. The man ignored him. Perhaps he couldn't hear him. The breeze was moving about a bit. It was only by chance that Arthur had heard the slight cough.

'Hello?' called Arthur. 'Hello!'

The man at last glanced round at him. He seemed surprised to see him. Arthur couldn't tell if he was surprised and pleased to see him or just surprised.

'Are you open?' called Arthur.

The man frowned in incomprehension. Arthur couldn't tell if he couldn't understand or couldn't hear.

'I'll pop over,' called Arthur. 'Don't go away.'

He clambered off the small platform and climbed quickly down the spiralling pegs, arriving at the bottom quite dizzy.

He started to make his way over to the pole on which the old man was sitting, and then suddenly realized that he had disoriented himself on the way down and didn't know for certain which one it was.

He looked around for landmarks and worked out which was the right one.

He climbed it. It wasn't.

'Damn,' he said. 'Excuse me!' he called out to the old

man again, who was now straight in front of him and forty feet away. 'Got lost. Be with you in a minute.' Down he went again, getting very hot and bothered.

When he arrived, panting and sweating, at the top of the pole that he knew for certain was the right one he realized that the man was, somehow or other, mucking him about.

'What do you want?' shouted the old man crossly at him. He was now sitting on top of the pole that Arthur recognized was the one that he had been on himself when eating his sandwich.

'How did you get over there?' called Arthur in bewilderment.

'You think I'm going to tell you just like that what it took me forty springs, summers and autumns of sitting on top of a pole to work out?'

'What about winter?'

'What about winter?'

'Don't you sit on the pole in the winter?'

'Just because I sit up a pole for most of my life,' said the man, 'doesn't mean I'm an idiot. I go south in the winter. Got a beach house. Sit on the chimney stack.'

'Do you have any advice for a traveller?'

'Yes. Get a beach house.'

'I see.'

The man stared out over the hot, dry scrubby landscape. From here Arthur could just see the old woman, a tiny speck in the distance, dancing up and down swatting flies.

'You see her?' called the old man, suddenly.

'Yes,' said Arthur. 'I consulted her, in fact.'

'Fat lot she knows. I got the beach house because she turned it down. What advice did she give you?'

'Do exactly the opposite of everything she's done.'

'In other words, get a beach house.'

'I suppose so,' said Arthur. 'Well, maybe I'll get one.'

'Hmmm.'

The horizon was swimming in a fetid heat haze.

'Any other advice?' asked Arthur. 'Other than to do with real estate?'

'A beach house isn't just real estate. It's a state of mind,' said the man. He turned and looked at Arthur.

Oddly, the man's face was now only a couple of feet away. He seemed in one way to be a perfectly normal shape, but his body was sitting cross-legged on a pole forty feet away while his face was only two feet from Arthur's. Without moving his head, and without seeming to do anything odd at all, he stood up and stepped on to the top of another pole. Either it was just the heat, thought Arthur, or space was a different shape for him.

'A beach house,' he said, 'doesn't even have to be on the beach. Though the best ones are. We all like to congregate,' he went on, 'at boundary conditions.'

'Really?' said Arthur.

'Where land meets water. Where earth meets air. Where body meets mind. Where space meets time. We like to be on one side, and look at the other.'

Arthur got terribly excited. This was exactly the sort of thing he'd been promised in the brochure. Here was a man who seemed to be moving through some kind of Escher space saying really profound things about all sorts of stuff.

It was unnerving though. The man was now stepping from pole to ground, from ground to pole, from pole to pole, from pole to horizon and back: he was making complete nonsense of Arthur's spatial universe. 'Please stop!' Arthur said, suddenly.

'Can't take it, huh?' said the man. Without the slightest movement he was now back, sitting cross-legged, on top of the pole forty feet in front of Arthur. 'You come to me for advice, but you can't cope with anything you don't recognize. Hmmm. So we'll have to tell you something you already know but make it sound like news, eh? Well, business as usual, I suppose.' He sighed and squinted mournfully into the distance.

'Where you from, boy?' he then asked.

Arthur decided to be clever. He was fed up with being mistaken for a complete idiot by everyone he ever met. 'Tell you what,' he said. 'You're a seer. Why don't you tell me?'

The old man sighed again. 'I was just,' he said, passing his hand round behind his head, 'making conversation.' When he brought his hand round to the front again, he had a globe of the Earth spinning on his up-pointed forefinger. It was unmistakable. He put it away again. Arthur was stunned.

'How did you—'

'I can't tell you.'

'Why not? I've come all this way.'

'You cannot see what I see because you see what you see. You cannot know what I know because you know what you know. What I see and what I know cannot be added to what you see and what you know because they are not of the same kind. Neither can it replace what you see and what you know, because that would be to replace you yourself.'

'Hang on, can I write this down?' said Arthur, excitedly fumbling in his pocket for a pencil.

'You can pick up a copy at the spaceport,' said the old man. 'They've got racks of the stuff.'

'Oh,' said Arthur, disappointed. 'Well, isn't there anything that's perhaps a bit more specific to me?'

'Everything you see or hear or experience in any way at all is specific to you. You create a universe by perceiving it, so everything in the universe you perceive is specific to you.'

Arthur looked at him doubtfully. 'Can I get that at the spaceport, too?' he said.

'Check it out,' said the old man.

'It says in the brochure,' said Arthur, pulling it out of his pocket and looking at it again, 'that I can have a special prayer, individually tailored to me and my special needs.'

'Oh, all right,' said the old man. 'Here's a prayer for you. Got a pencil?'

'Yes,' said Arthur.

'It goes like this. Let's see now: "Protect me from knowing what I don't need to know. Protect me from even knowing that there are things to know that I don't know. Protect me from knowing that I decided not to know about the things that I decided not to know about. Amen." That's it. It's what you pray silently inside yourself anyway, so you may as well have it out in the open.'

'Hmmm,' said Arthur. 'Well, thank you—'

'There's another prayer that goes with it that's very important,' continued the old man, 'so you'd better jot this down, too.'

'OK.'

'It goes, "Lord, lord, lord . . ." It's best to put that bit in, just in case. You can never be too sure. "Lord, lord, lord. Protect me from the consequences of the above prayer. Amen." And that's it. Most of the trouble people get into in life comes from missing out that last part.'

'Ever heard of a place called Stavromula Beta?' asked Arthur.

'No.'

'Well, thank you for your help,' said Arthur.

'Don't mention it,' said the man on the pole, and vanished.

10

Ford hurled himself at the door of the editor-in-chief's office, tucked himself into a tight ball as the frame splintered and gave way once again, rolled rapidly across the floor to where the smart grey crushed-leather sofa was and set up his strategic operational base behind it.

That, at least, was the plan.

Unfortunately the smart grey crushed-leather sofa wasn't there.

Why, thought Ford, as he twisted himself round in mid-air, lurched, dived and scuttled for cover behind Harl's desk, did people have this stupid obsession with rearranging their office furniture every five minutes?

Why, for instance, replace a perfectly serviceable if rather muted grey crushed-leather sofa with what appeared to be a small tank?

And who was the big guy with the mobile rocket launcher on his shoulder? Someone from head office? Couldn't be. This was head office. At least it was the head office of the *Guide*. Where these InfiniDim Enterprises guys came from Zarquon knew. Nowhere very sunny, judging from the slug-like colour and texture of their skins. This was all wrong, thought Ford. People connected with the *Guide* should come from sunny places.

There were several of them, in fact, and all of them seemed to be more heavily armed and armoured than you normally expected corporate executives to be, even in today's rough and tumble business world.

He was making a lot of assumptions here, of course. He was assuming that the big, bull-necked, slug-like guys were in some way connected with InfiniDim Enterprises, but it was a reasonable assumption and he felt happy about it because they had logos on their armour-plating which said 'InfiniDim Enterprises' on them. He had a nagging suspicion that this was not a business meeting, though. He also had a nagging feeling that these slug-like creatures were familiar to him in some way. Familiar, but in an unfamiliar guise.

Well, he had been in the room for a good two and a half seconds now, and thought that it was probably about time to start doing something constructive. He could take a hostage. That would be good.

Vann Harl was in his swivel chair, looking alarmed, pale and shaken. Had probably had some bad news as well as a nasty bang to the back of his head. Ford leapt to his feet and made a running grab for him.

Under the pretext of getting him into a good solid double underpinned elbow-lock, Ford managed surreptitiously to slip the Ident-i-Eeze back into Harl's inner pocket.

Bingo!

He'd done what he came to do. Now he just had to talk his way out of here.

'OK,' he said. 'I . . .' He paused.

The big guy with the rocket launcher was turning towards Ford Prefect and pointing it at him, which Ford couldn't help feeling was wildly irresponsible behaviour.

'I . . .' he started again, and then on a sudden impulse decided to duck.

There was a deafening roar as flames leapt from the back of the rocket launcher and a rocket leapt from its front.

The rocket hurtled past Ford and hit the large plate-glass window, which billowed outwards in a shower of a million shards under the force of the explosion. Huge shock waves of noise and air pressure reverberated around the room, sweeping a couple of chairs, a filing cabinet and Colin the security robot out of the window.

Ah! So they're not totally rocket-proof after all, thought Ford Prefect to himself. Someone should have a word with somebody about that. He disentangled himself from Harl and tried to work out which way to run.

He was surrounded.

The big guy with the rocket launcher was moving it up into position for another shot.

Ford was completely at a loss for what to do next.

'Look,' he said in a stern voice. But he wasn't certain how far saying things like 'Look' in a stern voice was necessarily going to get him, and time was not on his side. What the hell, he thought, you're only young once, and threw himself out of the window. That would at least keep the element of surprise on his side.

11

The first thing Arthur Dent had to do, he realized resignedly, was to get himself a life. This meant he had to find a planet he could have one on. It had to be a planet he could breathe on, where he could stand up and sit down without experiencing gravitational discomfort. It had to be somewhere where the acid levels were low and the plants didn't actually attack you.

'I hate to be anthropic about this,' he said to the strange thing behind the desk at the Resettlement Advice Centre on Pintleton Alpha, 'but I'd quite like to live somewhere where the people look vaguely like me as well. You know. Sort of human.'

The strange thing behind the desk waved some of its

stranger bits around and seemed rather taken aback by this. It oozed and glopped off its seat, thrashed its way slowly across the floor, ingested the old metal filing cabinet and then, with a great belch, excreted the appropriate drawer. It popped out a couple of glistening tentacles from its ear, removed some files from the drawer, sucked the drawer back in and vomited up the cabinet again. It thrashed its way back across the floor, slimed its way back up on to the seat and slapped the files on the table.

'See anything you fancy?' it asked.

Arthur looked nervously through some grubby and damp pieces of paper. He was definitely in some backwater part of the Galaxy here, and somewhere off to the left as far as the universe he knew and recognized was concerned. In the space where his own home should have been there was a rotten hick planet, drowned with rain and inhabited by thugs and boghogs. Even *The Hitchhiker's Guide to the Galaxy* seemed to work only fitfully here, which was why he was reduced to making these sorts of enquiries in these sorts of places. One place he always asked after was Stavromula Beta, but no one had ever heard of such a planet.

The available worlds looked pretty grim. They had little to offer him because he had little to offer them. He had been extremely chastened to realize that although he originally came from a world which had cars and computers and ballet and armagnac he didn't, by himself, know how any of it worked. He couldn't do it. Left to his own devices he couldn't build a toaster. He could just about make a sandwich and that was it. There was not a lot of demand for his services.

Arthur's heart sank. This surprised him, because he thought it was already about as low as it could possibly be. He closed his eyes for a moment. He so much wanted to be home. He so much wanted his own home world, the actual Earth he had grown up on, not to have been demolished. He so much wanted none of this to have happened. He so much wanted that when he opened his eyes again he would be standing on the doorstep of his little cottage in the West Country of England, that the sun would be shining over the green hills, the post van would be going up the lane, the daffodils would be blooming in his garden, and in the distance the pub would be opening for lunch. He so much wanted to take the newspaper down to the pub and read it over a pint of bitter. He so much wanted to do the crossword. He so much wanted to be able to get completely stuck on 17 across.

He opened his eyes.

The strange thing was pulsating irritably at him, tapping some kind of pseudopod on the desk.

Arthur shook his head and looked at the next sheet of paper.

Grim, he thought. And the next.

Very grim. And the next.

Oh . . . Now *that* looked better.

It was a world called Bartledan. It had oxygen. It had green hills. It even, it seemed, had a renowned literary culture. But the thing that most aroused his interest was a photograph of a small bunch of Bartledanian people, standing around in a village square, smiling pleasantly at the camera.

'Ah,' he said, and held the picture up to the strange thing behind the desk.

Its eyes squirmed out on stalks and rolled up and down the piece of paper, leaving a glistening trail of slime all over it.

'Yes,' it said with distaste. 'They do look exactly like you.'

*

Arthur moved to Bartledan and, using some money he had made by selling some toenail clippings and spit to a DNA bank, he bought himself a room in the village featured in the picture. It was pleasant there. The air was balmy. The people looked like him and seemed not to mind him being there. They didn't attack him with anything. He bought some clothes and a cupboard to put them in.

He had got himself a life. Now he had to find a purpose in it.

At first he tried to sit and read. But the literature of Bartledan, famed though it was throughout this sector of the Galaxy for its subtlety and grace, didn't seem to be able to sustain his interest. The problem was that it wasn't actually about human beings after all. It wasn't about what human beings wanted. The people of Bartledan were remarkably like human beings to look at, but when you said 'Good evening' to one, he would tend to look around with a slight sense of surprise, sniff the air and say that, yes, he supposed that it probably was a goodish evening now that Arthur came to mention it.

'No, what I meant was to wish you a good evening,' Arthur would say, or rather, used to say. He soon learned to avoid these conversations. 'I mean that I hope you have a good evening,' he would add.

More puzzlement.

'Wish?' the Bartledanian would say at last, in polite bafflement.

'Er, yes,' Arthur would then have said. 'I'm just expressing the hope that . . .'

'Hope?'

'Yes.'

'What is hope?'

Good question, thought Arthur to himself, and retreated back to his room to think about things.

On the one hand he could only recognize and respect

what he learnt about the Bartledanian view of the universe, which was that the universe was what the universe was, take it or leave it. On the other hand he could not help but feel that not to desire anything, not ever to wish or to hope, was just not natural.

Natural. There was a tricky word.

He had long ago realized that a lot of things that he had thought of as natural, like buying people presents at Christmas, stopping at red lights or falling at a rate of 32 feet per second per second, were just the habits of his own world and didn't necessarily work the same way anywhere else; but not to wish – that really couldn't be natural, could it? That would be like not breathing.

Breathing was another thing that the Bartledanians didn't do, despite all the oxygen in the atmosphere. They just stood there. Occasionally they ran around and played netball and stuff (without ever wishing to win though, of course – they would just play, and whoever won, won), but they never actually breathed. It was, for some reason, unnecessary. Arthur quickly learned that playing netball with them was just too spooky. Though they looked like humans, and even moved and sounded like humans, they didn't breathe and they didn't wish for things.

Breathing and wishing for things, on the other hand, was just about all that Arthur seemed to do all day. Sometimes he would wish for things so much that his breathing would get quite agitated, and he would have to go and lie down for a bit. On his own. In his small room. So far from the world which had given birth to him that his brain could not even process the sort of numbers involved without just going limp.

He preferred not to think about it. He preferred just to sit and read – or at least he would prefer it if there was anything worth reading. But nobody in Bartledanian stories ever wanted anything. Not even a glass of water. Certainly, they would fetch one if they were thirsty, but if there wasn't one available, they would think no more about it. He had just read an entire book in which the main character had, over the course of a week, done some work in his garden, played a great deal of netball, helped mend a road, fathered a child on his wife and then unexpectedly died of thirst just before the last chapter. In exasperation Arthur had combed his way back through the book and in the end had found a passing reference to some problem with the plumbing in Chapter 2. And that was it. So the guy dies. It just happens.

It wasn't even the climax of the book, because there wasn't one. The character died about a third of the way through the penultimate chapter of the book, and the rest of it was just more stuff about road-mending. The book just finished dead at the one hundred thousandth word, because that was how long books were on Bartledan.

Arthur threw the book across the room, sold the room and left. He started to travel with wild abandon, trading in more and more spit, toenails, fingernails, blood, hair, anything that anybody wanted, for tickets. For semen, he discovered, he could travel first class. He settled nowhere, but only existed in the hermetic, twilight world of the cabins of hyperspatial starships, eating, drinking, sleeping, watching movies, only stopping at spaceports to donate more DNA and catch the next long-haul ship out. He waited and waited for another accident to happen.

The trouble with trying to make the right accident happen is that it won't. That is not what 'accident' means. The accident that eventually occurred was not what he had planned at all. The ship he was on blipped in hyperspace, flickered horribly between ninety-seven different points in the Galaxy simultaneously, caught the unexpected gravitational pull of an uncharted planet in one of them, became ensnared in its outer atmosphere and began to fall, screaming and tearing, into it.

The ship's systems protested all the way down that everything was perfectly normal and under control, but when it went into a final hectic spin, ripped wildly through half a mile of trees and finally exploded into a seething ball of flame it became clear that this was not the case.

Fire engulfed the forest, boiled into the night, then neatly put itself out, as all unscheduled fires over a certain size are now required to do by law. For a short while afterwards, other small fires flared up here and there as odd pieces of scattered debris exploded quietly in their own time. Then they too died away.

Arthur Dent, because of the sheer boredom of endless interstellar flight, was the only one on board who had actually familiarized himself with the ship's safety procedures in case of an unscheduled landing, and was therefore the sole survivor. He lay dazed, broken and bleeding in a sort of fluffy pink plastic cocoon with 'Have a nice day' printed in over three thousand different languages all over it.

Black, roaring silences swam sickeningly through his shattered mind. He knew with a kind of resigned certainty that he would survive, because he had not yet been to Stavromula Beta.

After what seemed an eternity of pain and darkness, he became aware of quiet shapes moving around him.

12

Ford tumbled through the open air in a cloud of glass splinters and chair parts. Again, he hadn't really thought things through, really, and was just playing it by ear, buying time. At times of major crisis he found it was often quite helpful to have his life flash before his eyes. It gave him a chance to reflect on things, see things in some sort of perspective, and it sometimes furnished him with a vital clue as to what to do next.

There was the ground rushing up to meet him at 30 feet per second per second, but he would, he thought, deal with that problem when he got to it. First things first.

Ah, here it came. His childhood. Humdrum stuff, he'd been through it all before. Images flashed by. Boring times on Betelgeuse Five. Zaphod Beeblebrox as a kid. Yes he knew all that. He wished he had some kind of fast forward in his brain. His seventh birthday party, being given his first towel. Come on, come on.

He was twisting and turning downwards, the outside air at this height a cold shock to his lungs. Trying not to inhale glass.

Early voyages to other planets. Oh for Zark's sake, this was like some sort of bloody travelogue documentary before the main feature. First beginning to work for the *Guide*.

Ah!

Those were the days. They worked out of a hut on the Bwenelli Atoll on Fanalla before the Riktanarqals and the Danqueds vertled it. Half a dozen guys, some towels, a handful of highly sophisticated digital devices, and most importantly a lot of dreams. No. Most importantly a lot of Fanallan rum. To be completely accurate, that Ol' Janx Spirit was the absolute most important thing, then the Fanallan rum, and also some of the beaches on the atoll where the local girls would hang out, but the dreams were important as well. Whatever happened to those?

He couldn't quite remember what the dreams were, in fact, but they had seemed immensely important at the time. They had certainly not involved this huge towering office block he was now falling down the side of. All of that had come when some of the original team had started to settle down and get greedy, while he and others had stayed out in the field, researching and hitch hiking, and gradually becoming more and more isolated from the corporate nightmare the *Guide* had inexorably turned into, and the architectural monstrosity it had come to occupy. Where were the dreams in that? He thought of all the corporate lawyers who occupied half of the building, all the 'operatives' who occupied the lower levels, and all the sub-editors and their secretaries and their secretaries' lawyers and their secretaries' lawyers' secretaries, and worst of all the accountants and the marketing department.

He had half a mind just to keep on falling. Two fingers to the lot of them.

He was just passing the seventeenth floor now, where the marketing department hung out. Load of tosspots all arguing about what colour the *Guide* should be and exercising their infinitely infallible skills of being wise after the event. If any of them had chosen to look out of the window at that moment they would have been startled by the sight of Ford Prefect dropping past them to his certain death and flicking V-signs at them.

Sixteenth floor. Sub-editors. Bastards. What about all that copy of his they'd cut? Fifteen years of research he'd filed from one planet alone and they'd cut it to two words. 'Mostly harmless.' V-signs to them as well.

Fifteenth floor. Logistical Administration, whatever that was about. They all had big cars. That, he thought, was what that was about.

Fourteenth floor. Personnel. He had a very shrewd suspicion that it was they who had engineered his fifteen-year exile while the *Guide* metamorphosed into the corporate monolith (or rather, duolith – mustn't forget the lawyers) it had become.

Thirteenth floor. Research and development.

Hang about.

Thirteenth floor.

He was having to think rather fast at the moment because the situation was becoming a little urgent.

He suddenly remembered the floor display panel in the elevator. It hadn't had a thirteenth floor. He'd thought no more about it because, having spent fifteen years on the rather backward planet Earth where they were superstitious about the number thirteen, he was used to being in buildings that numbered their floors without it. No reason for that here, though.

The windows of the thirteenth floor, he could not help noticing as he flashed swiftly by them, were darkened.

What was going on in there? He started to remember all the stuff that Harl had been talking about. One, new, multidimensional *Guide* spread across an infinite number of universes. It had sounded, the way Harl had put it, like wild meaninglessness dreamed up by the marketing department with the backing of the accountants. If it was any more real than that then it was a very weird and dangerous idea. Was it real? What was going on behind the darkened windows of the sealed-off thirteenth floor?

Ford felt a rising sense of curiosity, and then a rising sense of panic. That was the complete list of rising feelings he had. In every other respect he was falling very rapidly. He really ought to turn his mind to wondering how he was going to get out of this situation alive.

He glanced down. A hundred feet or so below him people were milling around, some of them beginning to look up expectantly. Clearing a space for him. Even temporarily calling off the wonderful and completely fatuous hunt for wockets.

He would hate to disappoint them, but about two feet below him, he hadn't realized before, was Colin. Colin had obviously been happily dancing attendance and waiting for him to decide what he wanted to do.

'Colin!' Ford bawled.

Colin didn't respond. Ford went cold. Then he suddenly realized that he hadn't told Colin his name was Colin.

'Come up here!' Ford bawled.

Colin bobbed up beside him. Colin was enjoying the ride down immensely and hoped that Ford was, too.

Colin's world went unexpectedly dark as Ford's towel suddenly enveloped him. Colin immediately felt himself get much, much heavier. He was thrilled and delighted by the challenge that Ford had presented him with. Just not sure if he could handle it, that was all.

The towel was slung over Colin. Ford was hanging from the towel, gripping to its seams. Other hitchhikers had seen fit to modify their towels in exotic ways, weaving all kinds of esoteric tools and utilities and even computer equipment into their fabric. Ford was a purist. He liked to keep things simple. He carried a regular towel from a regular domestic soft furnishings shop. It even had a kind of blue and pink floral pattern despite his repeated attempts to bleach and stone wash it. It had a couple of pieces of wire threaded into it, a bit of flexible writing stick, and also some nutrients soaked into one of the corners of the fabric so he could suck it in an emergency, but otherwise it was a simple towel you could dry your face on.

The only actual modification he had been persuaded by a friend to make to it was to reinforce the seams.

Ford gripped the seams like a maniac.

They were still descending, but the rate had slowed.

'Up, Colin!' he shouted.

Nothing.

'Your name,' shouted Ford, 'is Colin. So when I shout "Up, Colin!" I want you, Colin, to go up. OK? Up, Colin!'

Nothing. Or rather a sort of muffled groaning sound from Colin. Ford was very anxious. They were descending very slowly now, but Ford was very anxious about the sort of people he could see assembling on the ground beneath him. Friendly, local, wocket-hunting types were dispersing, and thick, heavy, bull-necked, slug-like creatures with rocket launchers were, it seemed, sliding out of what was usually called thin air. Thin air, as all experienced Galactic travellers well know, is, in fact, extremely thick with multi-dimensional complexities.

'Up,' bellowed Ford again. 'Up! Colin, go up!'

Colin was straining and groaning. They were now more or less stationary in the air. Ford felt as if his fingers were breaking.

'Up!'

They stayed put.

'Up, up, up!'

A slug was preparing to launch a rocket at him. Ford couldn't believe it. He was hanging from a towel in mid-air and a slug was preparing to fire rockets at him. He was running out of anything he could think of doing and was beginning to get seriously alarmed.

This was the sort of predicament that he usually relied on having the *Guide* available for to give advice, however infuriating or glib, but this was not a moment for reaching into his pocket. And the *Guide* seemed to be no longer a friend and ally but was now itself a source of danger. These were the *Guide* offices he was hanging outside, for Zark's sake, in danger of his life from the people who now appeared to own the thing. What had become of all the dreams he vaguely remembered having on the Bwenelli Atoll? They should have let it all be. They should have stayed there. Stayed on the beach. Loved good women. Lived on fish. He should have known it was all wrong the moment they started hanging grand pianos over the sea-monster pool in the atrium. He began to feel thoroughly wasted and miserable. His fingers were on fire with clenched pain. And his ankle was still hurting.

Oh thank you, ankle, he thought to himself bitterly. Thank you for bringing up your problems at this time. I expect you'd like a nice warm footbath to make you feel better, wouldn't you? Or at least you'd like me to . . .

He had an idea.

The armoured slug had hoisted the rocket launcher up on to its shoulder. The rocket was presumably designed to hit anything in its path that moved.

Ford tried not to sweat because he could feel his grip on the seams of his towel slipping.

With the toe of his good foot he nudged and prised at the heel of the shoe on his hurting foot.

'Go *up*, damn you!' Ford muttered hopelessly to Colin, who was cheerily straining away but unable to rise. Ford worked away at the heel of his shoe.

He was trying to judge the timing, but there was no point. Just go for it. He only had one shot and that was it. He had now eased the back of his shoe down off his heel. His twisted ankle felt a little better. Well that was good, wasn't it?

With his other foot he kicked at the heel of the shoe. It slipped off his foot and fell through the air. About half a second later a rocket erupted up from the muzzle of its launcher, encountered the shoe falling through its path, went straight for it, hit it, and exploded with a great sense of satisfaction and achievement.

This happened about fifteen feet from the ground.

The main force of the explosion was directed downwards. Where, a second earlier, there had been a squad of InfiniDim Enterprises executives with a rocket launcher standing on an elegant terraced plaza paved with large slabs of lustrous stone cut from the ancient alabastrum quarries of Zentalquabula there was now, instead, a bit of a pit with nasty bits in it.

A great wump of hot air welled up from the explosion, throwing Ford and Colin violently up into the sky. Ford fought desperately and blindly to hold on and failed. He turned helplessly upwards through the sky, reached the peak of a parabola, paused and then started to fall again. He fell and fell and fell and suddenly winded himself badly on Colin, who was still rising.

He clasped himself desperately on to the small spherical robot. Colin slewed wildly through the air towards the tower of the *Guide* offices, trying delightedly to control himself and slow down.

The world span sickeningly round Ford's head as they span and twisted round each other and then, equally sickeningly, everything suddenly stopped.

Ford found himself deposited dizzily on a window ledge.

His towel fell past and he grabbed at it and caught it.

Colin bobbed in the air inches away from him.

Ford looked around himself in a bruised, bleeding and breathless daze. The ledge was only about a foot wide and he was perched precariously on it, thirteen storeys up.

Thirteen.

He knew they were thirteen storeys up because the windows were dark. He was bitterly upset. He had bought those shoes for some absurd price in a store on the Lower East Side in New York. He had, as a result, written an entire essay on the joys of great footwear, all of which had been jettisoned in the 'Mostly harmless' debacle. Damn everything.

And now one of the shoes was gone. He threw his head back and stared at the sky.

It wouldn't be such a grim tragedy if the planet in question hadn't been demolished, which meant that he wouldn't even be able to get another pair.

Yes, given the infinite sideways extension of probability there was, of course, an almost infinite multiplicity of planets Earth, but, when you came down to it, a major pair of shoes wasn't something you could just replace by mucking about in multidimensional space–time.

He sighed.

Oh well, he'd better make the best of it. At least it had saved his life. For the time being.

He was perched on a foot-wide ledge thirteen storeys up the side of a building and he wasn't at all sure that that was worth a good shoe.

He stared in woozily through the darkened glass.

It was as dark and silent as the tomb.

No. That was a ridiculous thing to think. He'd been to some great parties in tombs.

Could he detect some movement? He wasn't quite sure. It seemed that he could see some kind of weird, flapping shadow. Perhaps it was just blood dribbling over his eyelashes. He wiped it away. Boy, he'd love to have a farm somewhere, keep some sheep. He peered into the window again, trying to make out what the shape was, but he had the feeling, so common in today's universe, that he was looking into some kind of optical illusion and that his eyes were just playing silly buggers with him.

Was there a bird of some kind in there? Was that what they had hidden away up here on a concealed floor behind darkened, rocket-proof glass? Someone's aviary? There was certainly something flapping about in there, but it seemed like not so much a bird, more a kind of bird-shaped hole in space.

He closed his eyes, which he'd been wanting to do for a bit anyway. He wondered what the hell to do next. Jump? Climb? He didn't think there was going to be any way of breaking in. OK, the supposedly rocket-proof glass hadn't stood up, when it came to it, to an actual rocket, but then that had been a rocket that had been fired at very short range from inside, which probably wasn't what the engineers who designed it had had in mind. It didn't mean he was going to be able to break the window here by wrapping his fist in his towel and punching. What the hell, he tried it anyway and hurt his fist. It was just as well he couldn't get a good swing from where he was sitting or he might have hurt it quite badly. The building had been sturdily reinforced when it was completely rebuilt after the Frogstar attack, and was probably the most heavily armoured publishing company in the business, but there was always, he thought, some weakness in any system designed by a corporate committee. He had already found one of them. The engineers who designed the windows had not expected them to be hit by a rocket from short range from the inside, so the window had failed.

So, what would the engineers not be expecting someone sitting on the ledge outside the window to do?

He wracked his brains for a moment or so before he got it.

The thing they wouldn't be expecting him to do was to be there in the first place. Only an absolute idiot would be sitting where he was, so he was winning already. A common mistake that people make when trying to design something completely foolproof is to underestimate the ingenuity of complete fools.

He pulled his newly acquired credit card from his pocket, slid it into a crack where the window met its surrounding frame, and did something a rocket would not have been able to do. He wiggled it around a bit. He felt a catch slip. He slid the window open and almost fell backwards off the ledge laughing, giving thanks as he did so for the Great Ventilation and Telephone Riots of SrDt 3454.

The Great Ventilation and Telephone Riots of SrDt 3454 had started off as just a lot of hot air. Hot air was, of course, the problem that ventilation was supposed to solve and generally it had solved the problem reasonably well up to the point when someone invented air-conditioning, which solved the problem far more throbbingly.

And that was all well and good provided you could stand the noise and the dribbling until someone else came up with something even sexier and smarter than air-conditioning which was called in-building climate control.

Now this was quite something.

The major differences from just ordinary air-conditioning were that it was thrillingly more expensive, involved a huge amount of sophisticated measuring and regulating equipment which was far better at knowing, moment by moment, what kind of air people wanted to breathe than mere people did.

It also meant that, to be sure that mere people didn't muck up the sophisticated calculations which the system was making on their behalf, all the windows in the buildings were built sealed shut. This is true.

While the systems were being installed, a number of people who were going to work in the buildings found themselves having conversations with Breathe-O-Smart systems fitters which went something like this:

'But what if we want to have the windows open?'

'You won't want to have the windows open with new Breathe-O-Smart.'

'Yes but supposing we just wanted to have them open for a little bit?'

'You won't want to have them open even for a little bit. The new Breathe-O-Smart system will see to that.'

'Hmmm.'

'Enjoy Breathe-O-Smart!'

'OK, so what if the Breathe-O-Smart breaks down or goes wrong or something?'

'Ah! One of the smartest features of the Breathe-O-Smart is that it cannot possibly go wrong. So. No worries on that score. Enjoy your breathing now, and have a nice day.'

(It was, of course, as a result of the Great Ventilation and Telephone Riots of SrDt 3454, that all mechanical or electrical or quantum-mechanical or hydraulic or even wind, steam or piston-driven devices are now required to have a certain legend emblazoned on them somewhere. It doesn't matter how small the object is, the designers of the object have got to find a way of squeezing the legend in somewhere, because it is their attention which is being drawn to it rather than necessarily that of the user's.

The legend is this:

'The major difference between a thing that might go wrong and a thing that cannot possibly go wrong is that when a thing that cannot possibly go wrong goes wrong it usually turns out to be impossible to get at or repair.')

Major heat waves started to coincide, with almost magical precision, with major failures of the Breathe-O-Smart systems. To begin with this merely caused simmering resentment and only a few deaths from asphyxiation.

The real horror erupted on the day that three events happened simultaneously. The first event was that Breathe-O-Smart Inc. issued a statement to the effect that best results were achieved by using their systems in temperate climates.

The second event was the breakdown of a Breathe-O-Smart system on a particularly hot and humid day with the resulting evacuation of many hundreds of office staff into the street where they met the third event, which was a rampaging mob of long-distance telephone operators who had got so twisted with having to say, all day and every day, 'Thank you for using BS&S' to every single idiot who picked up a phone that they had finally taken to the streets with trash cans, megaphones and rifles.

In the ensuing days of carnage every single window in the city, rocket-proof or not, was smashed, usually to accompanying cries of 'Get off the line, asshole! I don't care what number you want, what extension you're calling from. Go and stick a firework up your bottom! Yeeehaah! Hoo Hoo Hoo! Veloooom! Squawk!' and a variety of other animal noises that they didn't get a chance to practise in the normal line of their work.

As a result of this, all telephone operators were granted a constitutional right to say 'Use BS&S and die!' at least once an hour when answering the phone and all office buildings were required to have windows that opened, even if only a little bit.

Another, unexpected result was a dramatic lowering

of the suicide rate. All sorts of stressed and rising executives who had been forced, during the dark days of the Breathe-O-Smart tyranny, to jump in front of trains or stab themselves, could now just clamber out on to their own window ledges and leap off at their leisure. What frequently happened, though, was that in the moment or two they had to look around and gather their thoughts they would suddenly discover that all they had really needed was a breath of air and a fresh perspective on things, and maybe also a farm on which they could keep a few sheep.

Another completely unlooked for result was that Ford Prefect, stranded thirteen storeys up a heavily armoured building armed with nothing but a towel and a credit card, was nevertheless able to clamber through a supposedly rocket-proof window to safety.

He closed the window neatly after him, having first allowed Colin to follow him through, and then started to look around for this bird thing.

The thing he realized about the windows was this: because they had been converted into openable windows *after* they had first been designed to be impregnable, they were, in fact, much less secure than if they had been designed as openable windows in the first place.

Hey ho, it's a funny old life, he was just thinking to himself, when he suddenly realized that the room he had gone to all this trouble to break into was not a very interesting one.

He stopped in surprise.

Where was the strange flapping shape? Where was anything that was worth all this palaver – the extraordinary veil of secrecy that seemed to lie over this room and the equally extraordinary sequence of events that had seemed to conspire to get him into it?

The room, like every other room in this building now,

was done out in some appallingly tasteful grey. There were a few charts and drawings on the wall. Most of them were meaningless to Ford, but then he came across something that was obviously a mock-up for a poster of some kind.

There was a kind of bird-like logo on it, and a slogan which said: '*The Hitchhiker's Guide to the Galaxy* Mk II: the single most astounding thing of any kind ever. Coming soon to a dimension near you.' No more information than that.

Ford looked around again. Then his attention was gradually drawn to Colin, the absurdly over-happy security robot, who was cowering in a corner of the room gibbering with what seemed strangely like fear.

Odd, thought Ford. He looked around to see what it was that Colin might have been reacting to. Then he saw something that he hadn't noticed before, lying quietly on top of a work bench.

It was circular and black and about the size of a small side plate. Its top and its bottom were smoothly convex so that it resembled a small lightweight throwing discus.

Its surfaces seemed to be completely smooth, unbroken and featureless.

It was doing nothing.

Then Ford noticed that there was something written on it. Strange. There hadn't been anything written on it a moment ago and now suddenly there was. There just didn't seem to have been any observable transition between the two states.

All it said, in small, alarming letters was a single word:

PANIC

A moment ago there hadn't been any marks or cracks in its surface. Now there were. They were growing.

Panic, the *Guide* Mk II said. Ford began to do as he

was told. He had just remembered why the slug-like creatures looked familiar. Their colour scheme was a kind of corporate grey, but in all other respects they looked exactly like Vogons.

13

The ship dropped quietly to land on the edge of the wide clearing, a hundred yards or so from the village.

It arrived suddenly and unexpectedly but with a minimum of fuss. One moment it was a perfectly ordinary late afternoon in the early autumn – the leaves were just beginning to turn red and gold, the river was beginning to swell again with the rains from the mountains in the north, the plumage of the pikka birds was beginning to thicken in anticipation of the coming winter frosts, any day now the Perfectly Normal Beasts would start their thunderous migration across the plains, and Old Thrashbarg was beginning to mutter to himself as he hobbled his way around the village, a muttering which meant that he was rehearsing and elaborating the stories that he would tell of the past year once the evenings had drawn in and people had no choice but to gather round the fire and listen to him and grumble and say that that wasn't how they remembered it – and the next moment there was a spaceship sitting there, gleaming in the warm autumn sun.

It hummed for a bit and then stopped.

It wasn't a big spaceship. If the villagers had been experts on spaceships they would have known at once that it was a pretty nifty one, a small sleek Hrundi four-berth runabout with just about every optional extra in the brochure except Advanced Vectoid Stabilisis, which only wimps went for. You can't get a good tight, sharp curve round a tri-lateral time axis with Advanced Vectoid Stabilisis. All right, it's a bit safer, but it makes the handling go all soggy.

The villagers didn't know all that, of course. Most of them here on the remote planet of Lamuella had never seen a spaceship, certainly not one that was all in one piece, and as it shone warmly in the evening light it was just the most extraordinary thing they had come across since the day Kirp caught a fish with a head at both ends.

Everybody had fallen silent.

Whereas a moment before two or three dozen people had been wandering about, chattering, chopping wood, carrying water, teasing the pikka birds, or just amiably trying to stay out of Old Thrashbarg's way, suddenly all activity died away and everybody turned to look at the strange object in amazement.

Or, not quite everybody. The pikka birds tended to be amazed by completely different things. A perfectly ordinary leaf lying unexpectedly on a stone would cause them to skitter off in paroxysms of confusion; sunrise took them completely by surprise every morning; but the arrival of an alien craft from another world simply failed to engage any part of their attention. They continued to *kar* and *rit* and *huk* as they pecked for seeds on the ground; the river continued with its quiet, spacious burbling.

Also, the noise of loud and tuneless singing from the last hut on the left continued unabated.

Suddenly, with a slight click and a hum, a door folded itself outwards and downwards from the spaceship. Then, for a minute or two, nothing further seemed to happen, other than the loud singing from the last hut on the left, and the thing just sat there.

Some of the villagers, particularly the boys, began to

edge forward a little bit to have a closer look. Old Thrashbarg tried to shoo them back. This was exactly the sort of thing that Old Thrashbarg didn't like to have happening. He hadn't foretold it, not even slightly, and even though he would be able to wrestle the whole thing into his continuing story somehow or other, it really was all getting a bit much to deal with.

He strode forward, pushed the boys back, and raised his arms and his ancient knobbly staff into the air. The long warm light of the evening sun caught him nicely. He prepared to welcome whatever gods these were as if he had been expecting them all along.

Still nothing happened.

Gradually it became clear that there was some kind of argument going on inside the craft. Time went by and Old Thrashbarg's arms were beginning to ache.

Suddenly the ramp folded itself back up again.

That made it easy for Thrashbarg. They were demons and he had repulsed them. The reason he hadn't foretold it was that prudence and modesty forbade.

Almost immediately a different ramp folded itself out on the other side of the craft from where Thrashbarg was standing, and two figures at last emerged on it, still arguing with each other and ignoring everybody, even Thrashbarg, whom they wouldn't even have noticed from where they were standing.

Old Thrashbarg chewed angrily on his beard.

To continue to stand there with his arms upraised? To kneel with his head bowed forward and his staff held out pointing at them? To fall backwards as if overcome in some titanic inner struggle? Perhaps just to go off to the woods and live in a tree for a year without speaking to anyone?

He opted just to drop his arms smartly as if he had done what he meant to do. They were really hurting so he didn't have much choice. He made a small, secret sign he had just invented towards the ramp which had closed and then made three and a half steps backwards, so he could at least get a good look at whoever these people were and then decide what to do next.

The taller one was a very good-looking woman wearing soft and crumply clothes. Old Thrashbarg didn't know this, but they were made of Rymplon™, a new synthetic fabric which was terrific for space travel because it looked its absolute best when it was all creased and sweaty.

The shorter one was a girl. She was awkward and sullen-looking, and was wearing clothes which looked their absolute worst when they were all creased and sweaty, and what was more she almost certainly knew it.

All eyes watched them, except for the pikka birds, which had their own things to watch.

The woman stood and looked around her. She had a purposeful air about her. There was obviously something in particular she wanted, but she didn't know exactly where to find it. She glanced from face to face among the villagers assembled curiously around her without apparently seeing what she was looking for.

Thrashbarg had no idea how to play this at all, and decided to resort to chanting. He threw back his head and began to wail, but was instantly interrupted by a fresh outbreak of song from the hut of the Sandwich Maker: the last one on the left. The woman looked round sharply, and gradually a smile came over her face. Without so much as a glance at Old Thrashbarg she started to walk towards the hut.

There is an art to the business of making sandwiches which it is given to few ever to find the time to explore in depth. It is a simple task, but the opportunities for satisfaction are many and profound: choosing the right bread, for instance. The Sandwich Maker had spent many months in daily consultation and experiment with Grarp the Baker and eventually they had between them created a loaf of exactly the consistency that was dense enough to slice thinly and neatly, while still being light, moist and having that fine nutty flavour which best enhanced the savour of roast Perfectly Normal Beast flesh.

There was also the geometry of the slice to be refined: the precise relationships between the width and height of the slice and also its thickness which would give the proper sense of bulk and weight to the finished sandwich: here again, lightness was a virtue, but so too were firmness, generosity and that promise of succulence and savour that is the hallmark of a truly intense sandwich experience.

The proper tools, of course, were crucial, and many were the days that the Sandwich Maker, when not engaged with the Baker at his oven, would spend with Strinder the Tool Maker, weighing and balancing knives, taking them to the forge and back again. Suppleness, strength, keenness of edge, length and balance were all enthusiastically debated, theories put forward, tested, refined, and many was the evening when the Sandwich Maker and the Tool Maker could be seen silhouetted against the light of the setting sun and the Tool Maker's forge making slow sweeping movements through the air trying one knife after another, comparing the weight of this one with the balance of another, the suppleness of a third and the handle binding of a fourth.

Three knives altogether were required. First there was the knife for the slicing of the bread: a firm, authoritative blade which imposed a clear and defining will on a loaf. Then there was the butter-spreading knife, which was a whippy little number but still with a firm backbone to it. Early versions had been a little too whippy, but now the combination of flexibility with a core of strength was exactly right to achieve the maximum smoothness and grace of spread.

The chief amongst the knives, of course, was the carving knife. This was the knife that would not merely impose its will on the medium through which it moved, as did the bread knife; it must work with it, be guided by the grain of the meat, to achieve slices of the most exquisite consistency and translucency, that would slide away in filmy folds from the main hunk of meat. The Sandwich Maker would then flip each sheet with a smooth flick of the wrist on to the beautifully proportioned lower bread slice, trim it with four deft strokes and then at last perform the magic that the children of the village so longed to gather round and watch with rapt attention and wonder. With just four more dexterous flips of the knife he would assemble the trimmings into a perfectly fitting jigsaw of pieces on top of the primary slice. For every sandwich the size and shape of the trimmings were different, but the Sandwich Maker would always effortlessly and without hesitation assemble them into a pattern which fitted perfectly. A second layer of meat and a second layer of trimmings, and the main act of creation would be accomplished.

The Sandwich Maker would pass what he had made to his assistant who would then add a few slices of newcumber and fladish and a touch of splagberry sauce, and then apply the topmost layer of bread and cut the sandwich with a fourth and altogether plainer knife. It was not that these were not also skilful operations, but they were lesser skills to be performed by a dedicated apprentice who would one day, when the Sandwich Maker finally laid down his tools, take over from him. It was an exalted position and that apprentice, Drimple, was the envy of his fellows. There were those in the village who were happy chopping wood, those who were content carrying water, but to be the Sandwich Maker was very heaven.

And so the Sandwich Maker sang as he worked.

He was using the last of the year's salted meat. It was a little past its best now, but still the rich savour of Perfectly Normal Beast meat was something unsurpassed in any of the Sandwich Maker's previous experience. Next week it was anticipated that the Perfectly Normal Beasts would appear again for their regular migration, whereupon the whole village would once again be plunged into frenetic action: hunting the Beasts, killing perhaps six, maybe even seven dozen of the thousands that thundered past. Then the Beasts must be rapidly butchered and cleaned, with most of the meat salted to keep it through the winter months until the return migration in the spring, which would replenish their supplies.

The very best of the meat would be roasted straight away for the feast that marked the Autumn Passage. The celebrations would last for three days of sheer exuberance, dancing and stories that Old Thrashbarg would tell of how the hunt had gone, stories that he would have been busy sitting making up in his hut while the rest of the village was out doing the actual hunting.

And then the very, very best of the meat would be saved from the feast and delivered cold to the Sandwich Maker. And the Sandwich Maker would exercise on it the skills that he had brought to them from the gods, and make the exquisite Sandwiches of the Third Season, of which the whole village would partake before beginning, the next day, to prepare themselves for the rigours of the coming winter.

Today he was just making ordinary sandwiches, if such delicacies, so lovingly crafted, could ever be called ordinary. Today his assistant was away so the Sandwich Maker was applying his own garnish, which he was happy to do. He was happy with just about everything in fact.

He sliced, he sang. He flipped each slice of meat neatly on to a slice of bread, trimmed it and assembled all the trimmings into their jigsaw. A little salad, a little sauce, another slice of bread, another sandwich, another verse of 'Yellow Submarine'.

'Hello, Arthur.'

The Sandwich Maker almost sliced his thumb off.

The villagers had watched in consternation as the woman had marched boldly to the hut of the Sandwich Maker. The Sandwich Maker had been sent to them by Almighty Bob in a burning fiery chariot. This, at least, was what Thrashbarg said, and Thrashbarg was the authority on these things. So, at least, Thrashbarg claimed, and Thrashbarg was . . . and so on and so on. It was hardly worth arguing about.

A few villagers wondered why Almighty Bob would send his onelie begotten Sandwich Maker in a burning fiery chariot rather than perhaps in one that might have landed quietly without destroying half the forest, filling it with ghosts and also injuring the Sandwich Maker quite badly. Old Thrashbarg said that it was the ineffable will of Bob, and when they asked him what ineffable meant he said look it up.

This was a problem because Old Thrashbarg had the only dictionary and he wouldn't let them borrow it. They asked him why not and he said that it was not for them to know the will of Almighty Bob, and when they asked him why not again he said because he said so. Anyway, somebody sneaked into Old Thrashbarg's hut one day while he was out having a swim and looked up 'ineffable'. 'Ineffable' apparently meant 'unknowable, indescribable, unutterable, not to be known or spoken about'. So that cleared that up.

At least they had got the sandwiches.

One day Old Thrashbarg said that Almighty Bob had decreed that he, Thrashbarg, was to have first pick of the sandwiches. The villagers asked him when this had happened, exactly, and Thrashbarg said it had happened yesterday, when they weren't looking. 'Have faith,' Old Thrashbarg said, 'or burn!'

They let him have first pick of the sandwiches. It seemed easiest.

And now this woman had just arrived out of nowhere, and gone straight for the Sandwich Maker's hut. His fame had obviously spread, though it was hard to know where to since, according to Old Thrashbarg, there wasn't anywhere else. Anyway, wherever it was she had come from, presumably somewhere ineffable, she was here now and was in the Sandwich Maker's hut. Who was she? And who was the strange girl who was hanging around outside the hut moodily and kicking at stones and showing every sign of not wanting to be there? It seemed odd that someone should come all the way from somewhere ineffable in a chariot that was obviously a vast improvement on the burning fiery one which had brought them the Sandwich Maker, if she didn't even want to be here.

They all looked to Thrashbarg, but he was on his knees mumbling and looking very firmly up into the sky and not catching anybody else's eye until he'd thought of something.

'Trillian!' said the Sandwich Maker, sucking his bleeding thumb. 'What . . .? Who . . .? When . . .? Where . . .?'

'Exactly the questions I was going to ask you,' said Trillian, looking around Arthur's hut. It was neatly laid out with his kitchen utensils. There were some fairly basic cupboards and shelves, and a basic bed in the corner. A door at the back of the room led to something Trillian couldn't see because the door was closed. 'Nice,' she said, but in an enquiring tone of voice. She couldn't quite make out what the set-up was.

'Very nice,' said Arthur. 'Wonderfully nice. I don't know when I've ever been anywhere nicer. I'm happy here. They like me, I make sandwiches for them, and . . . er, well that's it really. They like me and I make sandwiches for them.'

'Sounds, er . . .'

'Idyllic,' said Arthur, firmly. 'It is. It really is. I don't expect you'd like it very much, but for me it's, well, it's perfect. Look, sit down, please, make yourself comfortable. Can I get you anything, er, a sandwich?'

Trillian picked up a sandwich and looked at it. She sniffed it carefully.

'Try it,' said Arthur, 'it's good.'

Trillian took a nibble, then a bite and munched on it thoughtfully.

'It is good,' she said, looking at it.

'My life's work,' said Arthur, trying to sound proud and hoping he didn't sound like a complete idiot. He was used to being revered a bit, and was having to go through some unexpected mental gear changes.

'What's the meat in it?' asked Trillian.

'Ah yes, that's, um, that's Perfectly Normal Beast.'

'It's what?'

'Perfectly Normal Beast. It's a bit like a cow, or rather a bull. Kind of like a buffalo in fact. Large, charging sort of animal.'

'So what's odd about it?'

'Nothing, it's Perfectly Normal.'

'I see.'

'It's just a bit odd where it comes from.'

Trillian frowned, and stopped chewing.

'Where does it come from?' she asked with her mouth full. She wasn't going to swallow until she knew.

'Well, it's not just a matter of where it comes from, it's also where it goes to. It's all right, it's perfectly safe to swallow. I've eaten tons of it. It's great. Very succulent. Very tender. Slightly sweet flavour with a long dark finish.'

Trillian still hadn't swallowed.

'Where,' she said, 'does it come from, and where does it go to?'

'They come from a point just slightly to the east of the Hondo Mountains. They're the big ones behind us here, you must have seen them as you came in, and then they sweep in their thousands across the great Anhondo Plains and, er, well that's it really. That's where they come from. That's where they go.'

Trillian frowned. There was something she wasn't quite getting about this.

'I probably haven't made it quite clear,' said Arthur. 'When I say they come from a point to the east of the Hondo Mountains, I mean that that's where they suddenly appear. Then they sweep across the Anhondo Plains and, well, vanish really. We have about six days to catch as many of them as we can before they disappear. In the spring they do it again only the other way round, you see.'

Reluctantly, Trillian swallowed. It was either that or spit it out, and it did in fact taste pretty good.

'I see,' she said, once she had reassured herself that she didn't seem to be suffering any ill effects. 'And why are they called Perfectly Normal Beasts?'

'Well, I think because otherwise people might think it was a bit odd. I think Old Thrashbarg called them that. He says that they come from where they come from and they go to where they go to and that it's Bob's will and that's all there is to it.'

'Who . . . ?'

'Just don't even ask.'

'Well, you look well on it.'

'I feel well. You look well.'

'I'm well. I'm very well.'

'Well, that's good.'

'Yes.'

'Good.'

'Good.'

'Nice of you to drop in.'

'Thanks.'

'Well,' said Arthur, casting around himself. Astounding how hard it was to think of anything to say to someone after all this time.

'I expect you're wondering how I found you,' said Trillian.

'Yes!' said Arthur. 'I was wondering exactly that. How did you find me?'

'Well, as you may or may not know, I now work for one of the big Sub-Etha broadcasting networks that—'

'I did know that,' said Arthur, suddenly remembering. 'Yes, you've done very well. That's terrific. Very exciting. Well done. Must be a lot of fun.'

'Exhausting.'

'All that rushing around. I expect it must be, yes.'

'We have access to virtually every kind of information. I found your name on the passenger list of the ship that crashed.'

Arthur was astonished.

'You mean they *knew* about the crash?'

'Well, of course they knew. You don't have a whole spaceliner disappear without someone knowing about it.'

'But you mean, they knew where it had happened? They knew I'd survived?'

'Yes.'

'But nobody's ever been to look or search or rescue. There's been absolutely nothing.'

'Well, there wouldn't be. It's a whole complicated insurance thing. They just bury the whole thing. Pretend it never happened. The insurance business is completely screwy now. You know they've reintroduced the death penalty for insurance company directors?'

'Really?' said Arthur. 'No, I didn't. For what offence?'

Trillian frowned.

'What do you mean, offence?'

'I see.'

Trillian gave Arthur a long look, and then, in a new tone of voice, said, 'It's time for you to take responsibility, Arthur.'

Arthur tried to understand this remark. He found it often took a moment or so before he saw exactly what it was that people were driving at, so he let a moment or two pass at a leisurely rate. Life was so pleasant and relaxed these days, there was time to let things sink in. He let it sink in.

He still didn't quite understand what she meant, though, so in the end he had to say so.

Trillian gave him a cool smile and then turned back to the door of the hut.

'Random?' she called. 'Come in. Come and meet your father.'

14

As the *Guide* folded itself back into a smooth, dark disc, Ford realized some pretty hectic stuff. Or at least he tried to realize it, but it was too hectic to take in all in one go. His head was hammering, his ankle was hurting, and though he didn't like to be a wimp about his ankle, he always found that intense multi-dimensional logic was something he understood best in the bath. He needed time to think about this. Time, a tall drink, and some kind of rich, foamy oil.

He had to get out of here. He had to get the *Guide* out of here. He didn't think they'd make it together.

He glanced wildly round the room.

Think, think, think. It had to be something simple and obvious. If he was right in his nasty, lurking suspicion that he was dealing with nasty, lurking Vogons, then the more simple and obvious the better.

Suddenly he saw what he needed.

He wouldn't try to beat the system, he would just use it. The frightening thing about the Vogons was their absolute mindless determination to do whatever mindless thing it was they were determined to do. There was never any point in trying to appeal to their reason because they didn't have any. However, if you kept your nerve you could sometimes exploit their blinkered, bludgeoning insistence on being bludgeoning and blinkered. It wasn't merely that their left hand didn't always know what their right hand was doing, so to speak; quite often their right hand had a pretty hazy notion as well.

Did he dare just post the thing to himself?

Did he dare just put it in the system and let the Vogons work out how to get the thing to him while at the same time they were busy, as they probably would be, tearing the building apart to find out where he'd hidden it?

Yes.

Feverishly, he packed it. He wrapped it. He labelled it. With a moment's pause to wonder if he was really doing the right thing, he committed the package to the building's internal mail chute.

'Colin,' he said, turning to the little, hovering ball. 'I am going to abandon you to your fate.'

'I'm so happy,' said Colin.

'Make the most of it,' said Ford. 'Because what I want you to do is to nursemaid that package out of the building. They'll probably incinerate you when they find you, and I won't be here to help. It will be very, very nasty for you, and that's just too bad. Got it?'

'I gurgle with pleasure,' said Colin.

'Go!' said Ford.

Colin obediently dived down the mail chute in pursuit of his charge. Now Ford had only himself to worry about, but that was still quite a substantial worry. There were noises of heavy running footsteps outside the door, which he had taken the precaution of locking and shifting a large filing cabinet in front of.

He was worried that everything had gone so smoothly. Everything had fitted terribly well. He had hurtled through the day with reckless abandon and yet everything had worked out with uncanny neatness. Except for his shoe. He was bitter about his shoe. That was an account that was going to have to be settled.

With a deafening roar the door exploded inwards. In the turmoil of smoke and dust he could see large, slug-like creatures hurrying through.

So everything was going well was it? Everything was

working out as if the most extraordinary luck was on his side? Well, he'd see about that.

In a spirit of scientific enquiry he hurled himself out of the window again.

15

The first month, getting to know each other, was a little difficult. The second month, trying to come to terms with what they'd got to know about each other in the first month, was much easier.

The third month, when the box arrived, was very tricky indeed.

At the beginning, it was a problem even trying to explain what a month was. This had been a pleasantly simple matter for Arthur, here on Lamuella. The days were just a little over twenty-five hours long, which basically meant an extra hour in bed *every single day* and, of course, having regularly to reset his watch, which Arthur rather enjoyed doing.

He also felt at home with the number of suns and moons which Lamuella had – one of each – as opposed to some of the planets he'd fetched up on from time to time which had had ridiculous numbers of them.

The planet orbited its single sun every three hundred days, which was a good number because it meant the year didn't drag by. The moon orbited Lamuella just over nine times a year, which meant that a month was a little over thirty days, which was absolutely perfect because it gave you a little more time to get things done in. It was not merely reassuringly like Earth, it was actually rather an improvement.

Random, on the other hand, thought she was trapped

in a recurring nightmare. She would have crying fits and think the moon was out to get her. Every night it was there, and then, when it went, the sun came out and followed her. *Over and over again.*

Trillian had warned Arthur that Random might have some difficulty in adjusting to a more regular lifestyle than she had been used to up till now, but Arthur hadn't been ready for actual howling at the moon.

He hadn't been ready for any of this, of course.

His *daughter*?

His daughter? He and Trillian had never even – had they? He was absolutely convinced he would have remembered. What about Zaphod?

'Not the same species, Arthur,' Trillian had answered. 'When I decided I wanted a child they ran all sorts of genetic tests on me and could find only one match anywhere. It was only later that it dawned on me. I double checked and I was right. They don't usually like to tell you, but I insisted.'

'You mean you went to a DNA bank?' Arthur had asked, pop-eyed.

'Yes. But she wasn't quite as random as her name suggests, because, of course, you were the only *Homo sapiens* donor. I must say, though, it seems you were quite a frequent flyer.'

Arthur had stared wide-eyed at the unhappy looking girl who was slouching awkwardly in the door-frame looking at him.

'But when . . . how long . . .?'

'You mean, what age is she?'

'Yes.'

'The wrong one.'

'What do you mean?'

'I mean that I haven't any idea.'

'*What?*'

'Well, in my time line I think it's about ten years since I had her, but she's obviously quite a lot older than that. I spend my life going backwards and forwards in time, you see. The job. I used to take her with me when I could, but it just wasn't always possible. Then I used to put her into day care time zones, but you just can't get reliable time tracking now. You leave them there in the morning, you've simply no idea how old they'll be in the evening. You complain till you're blue in the face but it doesn't get you anywhere. I left her at one of the places for a few hours once, and when I came back she'd passed puberty. I've done all I can, Arthur, it's over to you. I've got a war to cover.'

The ten seconds that passed after Trillian left were about the longest of Arthur Dent's life. Time, we know, is relative. You can travel light-years through the stars and back, and if you do it at the speed of light then, when you return, you may have aged mere seconds while your twin brother or sister will have aged twenty, thirty, forty or however many years it is, depending on how far you travelled.

This will come to you as a profound personal shock, particularly if you didn't know you had a twin brother or sister. The seconds that you have been absent for will not have been sufficient time to prepare you for the shock of new and strangely distended family relationships when you return.

Ten seconds' silence was not enough time for Arthur to reassemble his whole view of himself and his life in a way that suddenly included an entire new daughter of whose merest existence he had had not the slightest inkling of a suspicion when he had woken that morning. Deep, emotional family ties cannot be constructed in ten seconds, however far and fast you travel away from them, and Arthur could only feel helpless, bewildered and numb as he looked at the girl standing in his doorway, staring at his floor.

He supposed that there was no point in pretending not to be hopeless. He walked over and he hugged her.

'I don't love you,' he said. 'I'm sorry. I don't even know you yet. But give me a few minutes.'

We live in strange times.

We also live in strange places: each in a universe of our own. The people with whom we populate our universes are the shadows of whole other universes intersecting with our own. Being able to glance out into this bewildering complexity of infinite recursion and say things like, 'Oh, hi, Ed! Nice tan. How's Carol?' involves a great deal of filtering skill for which all conscious entities have eventually to develop a capacity in order to protect themselves from the contemplation of the chaos through which they seethe and tumble. So give your kid a break, OK?

Extract from *Practical Parenting in a Fractally Demented Universe*

'What's this?'

Arthur had almost given up. That is to say, he was not going to give up. He was absolutely not going to give up. Not now. Not ever. But if he had been the sort of person who was going to give up, this was probably the time he would have done it.

Not content with being surly, bad-tempered, wanting to go and play in the Palaeozoic era, not seeing why they had to have the gravity on the whole time and shouting at the sun to stop following her, Random had also used his carving knife to dig up stones to throw at the pikka birds for looking at her like that.

Arthur didn't even know if Lamuella had had a

Palaeozoic era. According to Old Thrashbarg the planet had been found fully-formed in the navel of a giant earwig at four-thirty one Vroonday afternoon, and although Arthur, as a seasoned galactic traveller with good 'O' level passes in physics and geography, had fairly serious doubts about this, it was rather a waste of time trying to argue with Old Thrashbarg and there had never been much point before.

He sighed as he sat nursing the chipped and bent knife. He was going to love her if it killed him, or her, or both. It wasn't easy being a father. He knew that no one had ever said it was going to be easy, but that wasn't the point because he'd never asked about being one in the first place.

He was doing his best. Every moment that he could wrest away from making sandwiches he was spending with her, talking to her, walking with her, sitting on the hill with her watching the sun go down over the valley in which the village nestled, trying to find out about her life, trying to explain to her about his. It was a tricky business. The common ground between them, apart from the fact that they had almost identical genes, was about the size of a pebble. Or rather, it was about the size of Trillian and of her they had slightly differing views.

'What's this?'

He suddenly realized she had been talking to him and he hadn't noticed. Or rather he had not recognized her voice.

Instead of the usual tone of voice in which she spoke to him, which was bitter and truculent, she was just asking him a simple question.

He looked round in surprise.

She was sitting there on a stool in the corner of the hut in that rather hunched way she had, knees together, feet splayed out, with her dark hair hanging down over her face as she looked at something she had cradled in her hands.

Arthur went over to her, a little nervously.

Her mood swings were very unpredictable but so far they'd all been between different types of bad ones. Outbreaks of bitter recrimination would give way without warning to abject self-pity and then long bouts of sullen despair which were punctuated with sudden acts of mindless violence against inanimate objects and demands to go to electric clubs.

Not only were there no electric clubs on Lamuella, there were no clubs at all and, in fact, no electricity. There was a forge and a bakery, a few carts and a well, but those were the high-water mark of Lamuellan technology, and a fair number of Random's unquenchable rages were directed against the sheer incomprehensible backwardness of the place.

She could pick up Sub-Etha TV on a small Flex-O-Panel which had been surgically implanted in her wrist, but that didn't cheer her up at all because it was full of news of insanely exciting things happening in every other part of the Galaxy than here. It would also give her frequent news of her mother, who had dumped her to go off and cover some war which now seemed not to have happened, or at least to have gone all wrong in some way because of the absence of any proper intelligence gathering. It also gave her access to lots of great adventure shows featuring all sorts of fantastically expensive spaceships crashing into each other.

The villagers were absolutely hypnotized by all these wonderful magic images flashing over her wrist. They had only ever seen one spaceship crash, and it had been so frightening, violent and shocking and had caused so much horrible devastation, fire and death that, stupidly, they had never realized it was entertainment.

Old Thrashbarg had been so astonished by it that he

had instantly seen Random as an emissary from Bob, but had fairly soon afterwards decided that in fact she had been sent as a test of his faith, if not of his patience. He was also alarmed at the number of spaceship crashes he had to start incorporating into his holy stories if he was to hold the attention of the villagers, and not have them rushing off to peer at Random's wrist all the time.

At the moment she was not peering at her wrist. Her wrist was turned off. Arthur squatted down quietly beside her to see what she was looking at.

It was his watch. He had taken it off when he'd gone to shower under the local waterfall, and Random had found it and was trying to work it out.

'It's just a watch,' he said. 'It's to tell the time.'

'I know that,' she said. 'But you keep on fiddling with it, and it still doesn't tell the right time. Or even anything like it.'

She brought up the display on her wrist panel, which automatically produced a readout of local time. Her wrist panel had quietly got on with the business of measuring the local gravity and orbital momentum, and had noticed where the sun was and tracked its movement in the sky, all within the first few minutes of Random's arrival. It had then quickly picked up clues from its environment as to what the local unit conventions were and reset itself appropriately. It did this sort of thing continually, which was particularly valuable if you did a lot of travelling in time as well as space.

Random frowned at her father's watch, which didn't do any of this.

Arthur was very fond of it. It was a better one than he would ever have afforded himself. He had been given it on his twenty-second birthday by a rich and guilt-ridden godfather who had forgotten every single birthday he had had up till then, and also his name. It had the day, the date, the phases of the moon; it had

'To Albert on his twenty-first birthday' and the wrong date engraved on the battered and scratched surface of its back in letters that were still just about visible.

The watch had been through a considerable amount of stuff in the last few years, most of which would fall well outside the warranty. He didn't suppose, of course, that the warranty had especially mentioned that the watch was guaranteed to be accurate only within the very particular gravitational and magnetic fields of the Earth, and so long as the day was twenty-four hours long and the planet didn't explode and so on. These were such basic assumptions that even the lawyers would have missed them.

Luckily his watch was a wind-up one, or at least, a self-winder. Nowhere else in the Galaxy would he have found batteries of precisely the dimensions and power specifications that were perfectly standard on Earth.

'So what are all these numbers?' asked Random.

Arthur took it from her.

'These numbers round the edge mark the hours. In the little window on the right it says THU, which means Thursday, and the number is 14, which means it's the fourteenth day of the month of MAY which is what it says in this window over here.

'And this sort of crescent-shaped window at the top tells you about the phases of the moon. In other words it tells you how much of the moon is lit up at night by the sun, which depends on the relative positions of the sun and the moon and, well . . . the Earth.'

'The Earth,' said Random.

'Yes.'

'And that's where you came from, and where Mum came from.'

'Yes.'

Random took the watch back from him and looked at

it again, clearly baffled by something. Then she held it up to her ear and listened in puzzlement.

'What's that noise?'

'It's ticking. That's the mechanism that drives the watch. It's called clockwork. It's all kind of interlocking cogs and springs that work to turn the hands round at exactly the right speed to mark the hours and minutes and days and so on.'

Random carried on peering at it.

'There's something puzzling you,' said Arthur. 'What is it?'

'Yes,' said Random, at last. 'Why's it all in hardware?'

Arthur suggested they went for a walk. He felt there were things they should discuss, and for once Random seemed, if not precisely amenable and willing, then at least not growling.

From Random's point of view this was also all very weird. It wasn't that she wanted to be difficult, as such, it was just that she didn't know how or what else to be.

Who was this guy? What was this life she was supposed to lead? What was this world she was supposed to lead it in? And what was this universe that kept coming at her through her eyes and ears? What was it for? What did it want?

She'd been born in a spaceship that had been going from somewhere to somewhere else, and when it had got to somewhere else, somewhere else had only turned out to be another somewhere that you had to get to somewhere else again from, and so on.

It was her normal expectation that she was supposed to be somewhere else. It was normal for her to feel that she was in the wrong place.

Then, constant time travel had only compounded this problem, and had led to the feeling that she was not only always in the wrong place, but she was also almost always there at the wrong time.

She didn't notice that she felt this, because it was the only way she ever felt, just as it never seemed odd to her that nearly everywhere she went she needed either to wear weights or anti-gravity suits and usually special apparatus for breathing as well. The only places you could ever feel right were worlds you designed for yourself to inhabit – virtual realities in the electric clubs. It had never occurred to her that the real Universe was something you could actually fit into.

And that included this Lamuella place her mother had dumped her in. And it also included this person who had bestowed on her this precious and magical gift of life in return for a seat upgrade. It was just as well he had turned out to be rather kind and friendly or there would have been trouble. Really. She'd got a specially sharpened stone in her pocket she could cause a lot of trouble with.

It can be very dangerous to see things from somebody else's point of view without the proper training.

They sat on the spot that Arthur particularly liked, on the side of a hill overlooking the valley. The sun was going down over the village.

The only thing that Arthur wasn't quite so fond of was being able to see a little way into the next valley, where a deep dark mangled furrow in the forest marked the spot where his ship had crashed. But maybe that was what kept bringing him back here. There were plenty of spots from which you could survey the lush rolling countryside of Lamuella, but this was the one he was drawn to, with its nagging dark spot of fear and pain nestling just on the edge of his vision.

He had never been there again since he had been pulled out of the wreckage.

Wouldn't.

Couldn't bear it.

In fact he had gone some of the way back to it the very next day, while he was still numb and spinning with shock. He had a broken leg, a couple of broken ribs, some bad burns and was not really thinking coherently but had insisted that the villagers take him, which, uneasily, they had. He had not managed to get right to the actual spot where the ground had bubbled and melted, however, and had at last hobbled away from the horror for ever.

Soon, word had got around that the whole area was haunted and no one had ventured back there ever since. The land was full of beautiful, verdant and delightful valleys – no point in going to a highly worrying one. Let the past hold on to itself and let the present move forward into the future.

Random cradled the watch in her hands, slowly turning it to let the long light of the evening sun shine warmly in the scratches and scuffs of the thick glass. It fascinated her watching the spidery little second hand ticking its way round. Every time it completed a full circle, the longer of the two main hands had moved on exactly to the next of the sixty small divisions round the dial. And when the long hand had made its own full circle, the smaller hand had moved on to the next of the main digits.

'You've been watching it for over an hour,' said Arthur, quietly.

'I know,' she said. 'An hour is when the big hand has gone all the way round, yes?'

'That's right.'

'Then I've been watching it for an hour and seventeen . . . minutes.'

She smiled with a deep and mysterious pleasure and

moved very slightly so that she was resting just a little against his arm. Arthur felt a small sigh escape from him that had been pent up inside his chest for weeks. He wanted to put his arm around his daughter's shoulders, but felt it was too early yet and that she would shy away from him. But something was working. Something was easing inside her. The watch meant something to her that nothing in her life had so far managed to do. Arthur was not sure that he had really understood what it was yet, but he was profoundly pleased and relieved that something had reached her.

'Explain to me again,' said Random.

'There's nothing really to it,' said Arthur. 'Clockwork was something that developed over hundreds of years . . .'

'Earth years.'

'Yes. It became finer and finer and more and more intricate. It was highly skilled and delicate work. It had to be made very small, and it had to carry on working accurately however much you waved it around or dropped it.'

'But only on one planet?'

'Well, that was where it was made, you see. It was never expected to go anywhere else and deal with different suns and moons and magnetic fields and things. I mean the thing still *goes* perfectly well, but it doesn't really mean much this far from Switzerland.'

'From where?'

'Switzerland. That's where these were made. Small hilly country. Tiresomely neat. The people who made them didn't really know there were other worlds.'

'Quite a big thing not to know.'

'Well, yes.'

'So where did *they* come from?'

'They, that is we . . . we just sort of grew there. We

evolved on the Earth. From, I don't know, some kind of sludge or something.'

'Like this watch.'

'Um. I don't think the watch grew out of sludge.'

'You don't understand!'

Random suddenly leaped to her feet, shouting.

'You don't understand! You don't understand me, you don't understand *anything*! I *hate* you for being so stupid!'

She started to run hectically down the hill, still clutching the watch and shouting that she hated him.

Arthur jumped up, startled and at a loss. He started to run after her through the stringy and clumpy grass. It was hard and painful for him. When he had broken his leg in the crash, it had not been a clean break, and it had not healed cleanly. He was stumbling and wincing as he ran.

Suddenly she turned and faced him, her face dark with anger.

She brandished the watch at him. 'You don't understand that there's somewhere this belongs? Somewhere it works? Somewhere that it *fits*?'

She turned and ran again. She was fit and fleet-footed and Arthur could not remotely keep up with her.

It wasn't that he had not expected being a father to be this difficult, it was that he hadn't expected to be a father at all, particularly not suddenly and unexpectedly on an alien planet.

Random turned to shout at him again. For some reason he stopped each time she did.

'Who do you think I am?' she demanded angrily. 'Your upgrade? Who do you think Mum thought I was? Some sort of ticket to the life she didn't have?'

'I don't know what you mean by that,' said Arthur, panting and hurting.

'You don't know what anybody means by anything!'

'What do you mean?'

'Shut up! Shut up! Shut *up*!'

'Tell me! Please tell me! What does she mean by saying the life she didn't have?'

'She wished she'd stayed on Earth! She wished she hadn't gone off with that stupid brain-dead fruit gum, Zaphod! She thinks she would have had a different life!'

'But,' said Arthur, 'she would have been killed! She would have been killed when the world was destroyed!'

'That's a different life, isn't it?'

'That's . . .'

'She wouldn't have had to have me! She hates me!'

'You can't mean that! How could anyone possibly, er, I mean . . .'

'She had me because I was meant to make things fit for her. That was *my* job. But I fitted even worse than she did! So she just shut me off and carried on with her stupid life.'

'What's stupid about her life? She's fantastically successful, isn't she? She's all over time and space, all over the Sub-Etha TV networks . . .'

'Stupid! Stupid! Stupid! Stupid!'

Random turned and ran off again. Arthur couldn't keep up with her and at last he had to sit down for a bit and let the pain in his leg subside. The turmoil in his head he didn't know what to do with at all.

He hobbled into the village an hour later. It was getting dark. The villagers he passed said hello, but there was a sense of nervousness and of not quite knowing what was going on or what to do about it in the air. Old Thrashbarg had been seen pulling on his beard a fair bit and looking at the moon, and that was not a good sign either.

Arthur went into his hut.

Random was sitting hunched quietly over the table.

'I'm sorry,' she said. 'I'm so sorry.'

'That's all right,' said Arthur as gently as he knew how. 'It's good to, well, to have a little chat. There's so much we have to learn and understand about each other, and life isn't, well it isn't all just tea and sandwiches . . .'

'I'm *so* sorry,' she said again, sobbing.

Arthur went up to her and put his arm round her shoulder. She didn't resist or pull away. Then Arthur saw what it was she was so sorry about.

In the pool of light thrown by a Lamuellan lantern lay Arthur's watch. Random had forced the back off it with the back edge of the butter-spreading knife, and all of the minute cogs and springs and levers were lying in a tiny cock-eyed mess where she'd been fiddling with them.

'I just wanted to see how it worked,' said Random, 'how it all fitted together. I'm so sorry! I can't get it back together. I'm sorry, I'm sorry, I'm sorry. I don't know what to do. I'll get it repaired! Really! I'll get it repaired!'

The following day Thrashbarg came round and said all sorts of Bob stuff. He tried to exert a calming influence by inviting Random to let her mind dwell on the ineffable mystery of the giant earwig, and Random said there was no giant earwig and Thrashbarg went very cold and silent and said she would be cast into outer darkness. Random said good, she'd been born there, and the next day the parcel arrived.

This was all getting a bit eventful.

In fact, when the parcel arrived, delivered by a kind of robot drone that dropped out of the sky making droning robot noises, it brought with it a sense which gradually began to permeate through the whole village, that it was almost one event too many.

It wasn't the robot drone's fault. All it required was Arthur Dent's signature or thumb print, or just a few scrapings of skin cells from the nape of his neck and it would be on its way again. It hung around waiting, not quite sure what all this resentment was about. Meanwhile, Kirp had caught another fish with a head at both ends, but on closer inspection it turned out that it was in fact two fish cut in half and sewn together rather badly, so not only had Kirp failed to rekindle any great interest in two-headed fish but he had seriously cast doubt on the authenticity of the first one. Only the pikka birds seemed to feel that everything was exactly normal.

The robot drone got Arthur's signature and made its escape. Arthur bore the parcel back to his hut and sat and looked at it.

'Let's open it!' said Random, who was feeling much more cheerful this morning now that everything around her had got thoroughly weird, but Arthur said no.

'Why not?'

'It's not addressed to me.'

'Yes, it is.'

'No, it isn't. It's addressed to . . . well, it's addressed to Ford Prefect, in care of me.'

'Ford Prefect? Is he the one who . . . ?'

'Yes,' said Arthur tartly.

'I've heard about him.'

'I expect you have.'

'Let's open it anyway. What else are we going to do?'

'I don't know,' said Arthur, who really wasn't sure.

He had taken his damaged knives over to the forge bright and early that morning and Strinder had had a look at them and said that he would see what he could do.

They had tried the usual business of waving the knives through the air, feeling for the point of balance and the point of flex and so on, but the joy was gone from it, and Arthur had a sad feeling that his sandwich-making days were probably numbered.

He hung his head.

The next appearance of the Perfectly Normal Beasts was imminent, but Arthur felt that the usual festivities of hunting and feasting were going to be rather muted and uncertain. Something had happened here on Lamuella, and Arthur had a horrible feeling that it was him.

'What do you think it is?' urged Random, turning the parcel over in her hands.

'I don't know,' said Arthur. 'Something bad and worrying, though.'

'How do you know?' Random protested.

'Because anything to do with Ford Prefect is bound to be worse and more worrying than something that isn't,' said Arthur. 'Believe me.'

'You're upset about something, aren't you?' said Random.

Arthur sighed.

'I'm just feeling a little jumpy and unsettled, I think,' said Arthur.

'I'm sorry,' said Random, and put the package down again. She could see that it really would upset him if she opened it. She would just have to do it when he wasn't looking.

16

Arthur wasn't quite certain which he noticed as being missing first. When he noticed that the one wasn't there his mind instantly leapt to the other and he knew immediately that they were both gone and that something insanely bad and difficult to deal with would happen as a result.

Random was not there. And neither was the parcel.

He had left it up on a shelf all day, in plain view. It was an exercise in trust.

He knew that one of the things he was supposed to do as a parent was to show trust in his child, to build a sense of trust and confidence into the bedrock of relationship between them. He had had a nasty feeling that that might be an idiotic thing to do, but he did it anyway, and sure enough it had turned out to be an idiotic thing to do. You live and learn. At any rate, you live.

You also panic.

Arthur ran out of the hut. It was the middle of the evening. The light was getting dim and a storm was brewing. He could not see her anywhere, nor any sign of her. He asked. No one had seen her. He asked again. No one else had seen her. They were going home for the night. A little wind was whipping round the edge of the village, picking things up and tossing them around in a dangerously casual manner.

He found Old Thrashbarg and asked him. Thrashbarg looked at him stonily, and then pointed in the one direction that Arthur had dreaded, and had therefore instinctively known was the way she would have gone.

So now he knew the worst.

She had gone where she thought he would not follow her.

He looked up at the sky, which was sullen, streaked and livid, and reflected that it was the sort of sky that the Four Horsemen of the Apocalypse wouldn't feel like a bunch of complete idiots riding out of.

With a heavy sense of the utmost foreboding he set off on the track that led to the forest in the next valley. The first heavy blobs of rain began to hit the ground as Arthur tried to drag himself to some sort of run.

Random reached the crest of the hill and looked down into the next valley. It had been a longer and harder climb than she had anticipated. She was a little worried that doing the trip at night was not that great an idea, but her father had been mooching around near the hut all day trying to pretend to either her or himself that he wasn't guarding the parcel. At last he'd had to go over to the forge to talk with Strinder about the knives, and Random had seized her opportunity and done a runner with the parcel.

It was perfectly clear that she couldn't just open the thing there, in the hut, or even in the village. He might have come across her at any moment. Which meant that she had to go where she wouldn't be followed.

She could stop where she was now. She had gone this way in the hope that he wouldn't follow her, and even if he did he would never find her up in the wooded parts of the hill with night drawing in and the rain starting.

All the way up, the parcel had been jiggling under her arm. It was a satisfyingly hunky sort of thing: a box with a square top about the length of her forearm on each side, and about the length of her hand deep, wrapped up in brown plasper with an ingenious new form of self-knotting string. It didn't rattle as she shook it, but she sensed that its weight was concentrated excitingly at the centre.

Having come so far, though, there was a certain satisfaction in not stopping here, but carrying on down into what seemed to be almost a forbidden area – where her father's ship had come down. She wasn't exactly certain what the word 'haunted' meant, but it might be fun to find out. She would keep going and save the parcel up for when she got there.

It was getting darker, though. She hadn't used her tiny electric torch yet, because she didn't want to be visible from a distance. She would have to use it now, but it probably didn't matter since she would be on the other side of the hill which divided the valleys from each other.

She turned her torch on. Almost at the same moment a fork of lightning ripped across the valley into which she was heading and startled her considerably. As the darkness shuddered back around her and a clap of thunder rolled out across the land she felt suddenly rather small and lost with just a feeble pencil of light bobbing in her hand. Perhaps she should stop after all and open the parcel here. Or maybe she should go back and come out again tomorrow. It was only a momentary hesitation, though. She knew there was no going back tonight, and sensed that there was no going back ever.

She headed on down the side of the hill. The rain was beginning to pick up now. Where a short while ago it had been a few heavy blobs it was settling in for a good pour now, hissing in the trees, and the ground was getting slippery under her feet.

At least, she thought it was the rain hissing in the trees. Shadows were leaping and leering at her as her light bobbed through the trees. Onwards and downwards.

She hurried on for another ten or fifteen minutes, soaked to the skin now and shivering, and gradually became aware that there seemed to be some other light somewhere ahead of her. It was very faint and she wasn't certain if she was imagining it or not. She turned off her torch to see. There did seem to be some sort of dim glow ahead. She couldn't tell what it was. She turned her torch back on and continued down the hill, towards whatever it was.

There was something wrong with the woods, though. She couldn't immediately say what it was, but they didn't seem like sprightly healthy woods looking forward to a good spring. The trees were lolling at sickly angles and had a sort of pallid, blighted look about them. Random more than once had the worrying sensation that they were trying to reach towards her as she passed them, but it was just a trick of the way that her light caused their shadows to flicker and lurch.

Suddenly something fell out of a tree in front of her. She leapt backwards with alarm, dropping both the torch and the box as she did so. She went down into a crouch, pulling the specially sharpened rock out of her pocket.

The thing that had fallen out of the tree was moving. The torch was lying on the ground and pointing towards it, and a vast, grotesque shadow was slowly lurching through the light towards her. She could hear faint rustling and screeching noises over the steady hiss of the rain. She scrabbled on the ground for the torch, found it, and shone it directly at the creature.

At the same moment another dropped from a tree just a few feet away. She swung the torch wildly from one to another. She held her rock up, ready to throw.

They were quite small in fact. It was the angle of the light that had made them loom so large. Not only small, but small, furry and cuddly. And there was another, dropping from the trees. It fell through the beam of light, so she saw it quite clearly.

It fell neatly and precisely, turned, and then, like the other two, started slowly and purposefully to advance on Random.

She stayed rooted to the spot. She still had her rock poised and ready to throw, but was increasingly conscious of the fact that the things she had it poised and ready to throw at were squirrels. Or at least, squirrel-like things. Soft, warm, cuddly squirrel-like things advancing on her in a way she wasn't at all certain she liked.

She shone her torch directly on the first of them. It was making aggressive, hectoring, screeching noises, and carrying in one of its little fists a small tattered piece of wet, pink rag. Random hefted her rock menacingly in her hand, but it made no impression at all on the squirrel advancing on her with its wet piece of rag.

She backed away. She didn't know at all how to deal with this. If they had been vicious snarling slavering beasts with glistening fangs she would have pitched into them with a will, but squirrels behaving like this she couldn't quite handle.

She backed away again. The second squirrel was starting to make a flanking manoeuvre round to her right. Carrying a cup. Some kind of acorn thing. The third was right behind it and making its own advance. What was it carrying? Some little scrap of soggy paper, Random thought.

She stepped back again, caught her ankle against the root of a tree and fell over backwards.

Instantly the first squirrel darted forward and was on top of her, advancing along her stomach with cold purpose in its eyes, and a piece of wet rag in its fist.

Random tried to jump up, but only managed to jump about an inch. The startled movement of the squirrel on her stomach startled her in return. The squirrel froze, gripping her skin through her soaking shirt with its tiny claws. Then slowly, inch by inch, it made its way up her, stopped, and proffered her the rag.

She felt almost hypnotized by the strangeness of the thing and its tiny glinting eyes. It proffered her the rag again. It pushed it at her repeatedly, screeching insistently, till at last, nervously, hesitantly, she took the thing from it. It continued to watch her intently, its eyes darting all over her face. She had no idea what to do. Rain and mud were streaming down her face and she had a squirrel sitting on her. She wiped some mud out of her eyes with the rag.

The squirrel shrieked triumphantly, grabbed the rag back, leapt off her, ran scampering into the dark, enclosing night, darted up into a tree, dived into a hole in the trunk, settled back and lit a cigarette.

Meanwhile Random was trying to fend off the squirrel with the acorn cup full of rain and the one with the paper. She shuffled backwards on her bottom.

'No!' she shouted. 'Go away!'

They darted back, in fright, and then darted right forward again with their gifts. She brandished her rock at them. 'Go!' she yelled.

The squirrels scampered round in consternation. Then one darted straight at her, dropped the acorn cup in her lap, turned and ran off into the night. The other stood quivering for a moment, then put its scrap of paper neatly down in front of her and disappeared as well.

She was alone again, but trembling with confusion. She got unsteadily to her feet, picked up her rock and her parcel, then paused and picked up the scrap of paper as well. It was so soggy and dilapidated it was hard to make out what it was. It seemed just to be a fragment of an in-flight magazine.

Just as Random was trying to understand exactly

what it was that this all meant, a man walked out into the clearing in which she was standing, raised a vicious-looking gun and shot her.

Arthur was thrashing around hopelessly two or three miles behind her, on the upward side of the hill.

Within minutes of setting out he had gone back again and equipped himself with a lamp. Not an electric one. The only electric light in the place was the one that Random had brought with her. This was a kind of dim hurricane lamp: a perforated metal canister from Strinder's forge, which contained a reservoir of inflammable fish oil, a wick of knotted dried grass and was wrapped in a translucent film made from dried membranes from the gut of a Perfectly Normal Beast.

It had now gone out.

Arthur jiggled around with it in a thoroughly pointless kind of a way for a few seconds. There was clearly no way he was going to get the thing suddenly to burst into flame again in the middle of a rainstorm, but it's impossible not to make a token effort. Reluctantly he threw the thing aside.

What to do? This was hopeless. He was absolutely sodden, his clothes heavy and billowing with the rain, and now he was lost in the dark as well.

For a brief second he was lost in the blinding light, and then he was lost in the dark again.

The sheet of lightning had at least shown him that he was very close to the brow of the hill. Once he had breasted that he would . . . well, he wasn't certain what he would do. He'd have to work that out when he got there.

He limped forward and upwards.

A few minutes later he knew that he was standing panting at the top. There was some kind of dim glow in the distance below him. He had no idea what it was, and indeed he hardly liked to think. It was the only thing he had to make towards, though, so he started to make his way, stumbling, lost and frightened towards it.

The flash of lethal light passed straight through Random and, about two seconds later, so did the man who had shot it. Other than that he paid her no attention whatsoever. He had shot someone standing behind her, and when she turned to look, he was kneeling over the body and going through its pockets.

The tableau froze and vanished. It was replaced a second later by a giant pair of teeth framed by immense and perfectly glossed red lips. A huge blue brush appeared out of nowhere and started foamily to scrub at the teeth, which continued to hang there gleaming in the shimmering curtain of rain.

Random blinked at it twice before she got it.

It was a commercial. The guy who had shot her was part of a holographic in-flight movie. She must now be very close to where the ship had crashed. Obviously some of its systems were more indestructible than others.

The next half-mile of the journey was particularly troublesome. Not only did she have the cold and the rain and the night to contend with, but also the fractured and thrashing remains of the ship's on-board entertainment system. Spaceships and jetcars and helipods crashed and exploded continuously around her, illuminating the night, villainous people in strange hats smuggled dangerous drugs through her, and the combined orchestra and chorus of the Hallapolis State Opera performed the closing March of the AnjaQantine Star Guard from Act IV of Rizgar's *Blamwellamum of Woont* in a little glade somewhere off to her left.

And then she was standing on the lip of a very nasty

looking and bubbly edged crater. There was still a faint warm glow coming from what would otherwise have looked like an enormous piece of caramelized chewing gum in the centre of the pit: the melted remains of a great spaceship.

She stood looking at it for a longish while, and then at last started to walk along and around the edge of the crater. She was no longer certain what she was looking for, but kept moving anyway, keeping the horror of the pit to her left.

The rain was beginning to ease off a little, but it was still extremely wet, and since she didn't know what it was that was in the box, whether it was perhaps something delicate or damageable, she thought she ought to find somewhere reasonably dry to open it. She hoped she hadn't already damaged it by dropping it.

She played her torch around the surrounding trees, which were thin on the ground here, and mostly charred and broken. In the middle distance she thought she could see a jumbled outcrop of rock which might provide some shelter, and she started to pick her way towards it. All around she found the detritus that had been ejected from the ship as it broke up, before the final fireball.

After she had moved two or three hundred yards from the edge of the crater she came across the tattered fragments of some fluffy pink material, sodden, muddied and drooping amongst the broken trees. She guessed, correctly, that this must be the remains of the escape cocoon that had saved her father's life. She went and looked at it more closely, and then noticed something close to it on the ground, half covered in mud.

She picked it up and wiped the mud off it. It was some kind of electronic device the size of a small book. Feebly glowing on its cover, in response to her touch, were some large friendly letters. They said DON'T

PANIC. She knew what this was. It was her father's copy of *The Hitchhiker's Guide to the Galaxy*.

She felt instantly reassured by it, turned her head up to the thundery sky and let some rain wash over her face and into her mouth.

She shook her head and hurried on towards the rocks. Clambering up and over them she almost immediately found the perfect thing. The mouth of a cave. She played her torch into its interior. It seemed to be dry and safe. Picking her way carefully, she walked in. It was quite spacious, but didn't go that deep. Exhausted and relieved she sat on a convenient rock, put the box down in front of her and started immediately to open it.

17

For a long period of time there was much speculation and controversy about where the so-called 'missing matter' of the Universe had got to. All over the Galaxy the science departments of all the major universities were acquiring more and more elaborate equipment to probe and search the hearts of distant galaxies, and then the very centre and the very edges of the whole Universe, but when eventually it was tracked down it turned out in fact to be all the stuff which the equipment had been packed in.

There was quite a large quantity of missing matter in the box, little soft round white pellets of missing matter, which Random discarded for future generations of physicists to track down and discover all over again once the findings of the current generation of physicists had been lost and forgotten about.

Out of the pellets of missing matter she lifted the featureless black disc. She put it down on a rock beside her and sifted amongst all the missing matter to see if there was anything else, a manual or some attachments or something, but there was nothing else at all. Just the black disc.

She shone the torch on it.

As she did so, cracks began to appear along its apparently featureless surface. Random backed away nervously, but then saw that the thing, whatever it was, was merely unfolding itself.

The process was wonderfully beautiful. It was extraordinarily elaborate but also simple and elegant. It was like a piece of self-opening origami, or a rosebud blooming into a rose in just a few seconds.

Where just a few moments earlier there had been a smoothly curved black disc there was now a bird. A bird, hovering there.

Random continued to back away from it, carefully and watchfully.

It was a little like a pikka bird, only rather smaller. That is to say, in fact it was larger, or to be more exact, precisely the same size or, at least, not less than twice the size. It was also both a lot bluer and a lot pinker than pikka birds, while at the same time being perfectly black.

There was also something very odd about it, which Random couldn't immediately make out.

It certainly shared with pikka birds the impression it gave that it was watching something that you couldn't see.

Suddenly it vanished.

Then, just as suddenly everything went black. Random dropped into a tense crouch, feeling for the specially sharpened rock in her pocket again. Then the blackness receded and rolled itself up into a ball and then the blackness was the bird again. It hung in the air in front of her, beating its wings slowly and staring at her.

'Excuse me,' it said suddenly, 'I just have to calibrate myself. Can you hear me when I say this?'

'When you say what?' demanded Random.

'Good,' said the bird. 'And can you hear me when I say this?' It spoke this time at a much higher pitch.

'Yes, of course I can!' said Random.

'And can you hear me when I say this?' it said, this time in a sepulchrally deep voice.

'Yes!'

There was then a pause.

'No, obviously not,' said the bird after a few seconds. 'Good, well your hearing range is obviously between 20 and 16 KHz. So. Is this comfortable for you?' it said in a pleasant light tenor. 'No uncomfortable harmonics screeching away in the upper register? Obviously not. Good. I can use those as data channels. Now. How many of me can you see?'

Suddenly the air was full of nothing but interlocking birds. Random was well used to spending time in virtual realities, but this was something far weirder than anything she had previously encountered. It was as if the whole geometry of space was redefined in seamless bird shapes.

Random gasped and flung her arms round her face, her arms moving through bird-shaped space.

'Hmmm, obviously way too many,' said the bird. 'How about now?'

It concertina-ed into a tunnel of birds, as if it was a bird caught between parallel mirrors, reflecting infinitely into the distance.

'What are you?' shouted Random.

'We'll come to that in a minute,' said the bird. 'Just how many, please?'

'Well, you're sort of . . .' Random gestured helplessly off into the distance.

'I see, still infinite in extent, but at least we're homing in on the right dimensional matrix. Good. No, the answer is an *orange* and two lemons.'

'Lemons?'

'If I have three lemons and three oranges and I lose two oranges and a lemon what do I have left?'

'Huh?'

'OK, so you think that time flows *that* way, do you? Interesting. Am I still infinite?' it asked, ballooning this way and that in space. 'Am I infinite now? How yellow am I?'

Moment by moment the bird was going through mind-mangling transformations of shape and extent.

'I can't . . .' said Random, bewildered.

'You don't have to answer, I can tell from watching you now. So. Am I your mother? Am I a rock? Do I seem huge, squishy and sinuously intertwined? No? How about now? Am I going backwards?'

For once the bird was perfectly still and steady.

'No,' said Random.

'Well, I was in fact, I was moving backwards in time. Hmmm. Well, I think we've sorted all that out now. If you'd like to know, I can tell you that in your universe you move freely in three dimensions that you call space. You move in a straight line in a fourth, which you call time, and stay rooted to one place in a fifth, which is the first fundamental of probability. After that it gets a bit complicated, and there's all sorts of stuff going on in dimensions thirteen to twenty-two that you really wouldn't want to know about. All you really need to know for the moment is that the universe is a lot more complicated than you might think, even if you start from a position of thinking it's pretty damn complicated in the first place. I can easily not say words like "damn" if it offends you.'

'Say what you damn well like.'

'I will.'

'What the hell are you?' demanded Random.

'I am the *Guide*. In *your* universe I am *your Guide*. In fact I inhabit what is technically known as the Whole Sort of General Mish Mash, which means . . . well, let me show you.'

It turned in mid-air and swooped out of the cave, and then perched on a rock, just beneath an overhang, out of the rain, which was getting heavier again.

'Come on,' it said, 'watch this.'

Random didn't like being bossed around by a bird, but she followed it to the mouth of the cave anyway, still fingering the rock in her pocket.

'Rain,' said the bird. 'You see? Just rain.'

'I know what rain is.'

Sheets of the stuff were sweeping through the night, moonlight sifting through it.

'So what is it?'

'What do you mean, what is it? Look, who are you? What were you doing in that box? Why have I spent a night running through the forest fending off demented squirrels to find that all I've got at the end of it is a bird asking me what rain is? It's just water falling through the bloody air, that's what it is. Anything else you want to know or can we go home now?'

There was a long pause before the bird answered, 'You want to go home?'

'I haven't got a home!' Random almost shocked herself, she screamed the words so loudly.

'Look into the rain . . .' said the bird *Guide*.

'I'm looking into the rain! What else is there to look at?'

'What do you see?'

'What do you mean, you stupid bird? I just see a load of rain. It's just water, falling.'

'What shapes do you see in the water?'

'Shapes? There aren't any shapes. It's just, just . . .'

'Just a mish mash,' said the bird *Guide*.

'Yes . . .'

'Now what do you see?'

Just on the very edge of visibility a thin faint beam fanned out of the bird's eyes. In the dry air beneath the overhang there was nothing to see. Where the beam hit the drops of rain as they fell through it, there was a flat sheet of light, so bright and vivid it seemed solid.

'Oh great. A laser show,' said Random fractiously. 'Never seen one of *those* before, of course, except at about five million rock concerts.'

'Tell me what you see!'

'Just a flat sheet! Stupid bird.'

'There's nothing there that wasn't there before. I'm just using light to draw your attention to certain drops at certain moments. Now what do you see?'

The light shut off.

'Nothing.'

'I'm doing exactly the same thing, but with ultraviolet light. You can't see it.'

'So what's the point of showing me something I can't see?'

'So that you understand that just because you see something, it doesn't mean to say it's there. And if you don't see something it doesn't mean to say it's not there, it's only what your senses bring to your attention.'

'I'm bored with this,' said Random, and then gasped.

Hanging in the rain was a giant and very vivid three-dimensional image of her father looking startled about something.

*

About two miles away behind Random, her father, struggling his way through the woods suddenly stopped. He was startled to see an image of himself looking startled about something hanging brightly in the rain-filled air about two miles away. About two miles away some distance to the right of the direction in which he was heading.

He was almost completely lost, convinced he was going to die of cold and wet and exhaustion and beginning to wish he could just get on with it. He had just been brought an entire golfing magazine by a squirrel, as well, and his brain was beginning to howl and gibber.

Seeing a huge bright image of himself light up in the sky told him that, on balance, he was probably right to howl and gibber but probably wrong as far as the direction he was heading was concerned.

Taking a deep breath, he turned and headed off towards the inexplicable light show.

'OK, so what's that supposed to prove?' demanded Random. It was the fact that the image was her father that had startled her rather than the appearance of the image itself. She had seen her first hologram when she was two months old and had been put in it to play. She had seen her most recent one about half an hour ago playing the March of the AnjaQantine Star Guard.

'Only that it's no more there or not there than the sheet was,' said the bird. 'It's just the interaction of water from the sky moving in one direction, with light at frequencies your senses can detect moving in another. It makes an apparently solid image in your mind. But it's all just images in the Mish Mash. Here's another one for you.'

'My mother!' said Random.

'No,' said the bird.

'I know my mother when I see her!'

The image was of a woman emerging from a spacecraft inside a large, grey hangar-like building. She was being escorted by a group of tall, thin purplish-green creatures. It was definitely Random's mother. Well, almost definitely. Trillian wouldn't have been walking quite so uncertainly in low gravity, or looking around her at a boring old life-support environment with quite such a disbelieving look on her face, or carrying such a quaint old camera.

'So who is it?' demanded Random.

'She is part of the extent of your mother on the probability axis,' said the bird *Guide*.

'I haven't the faintest idea what you mean.'

'Space, time and probability all have axes along which it is possible to move.'

'Still dunno. Though I think . . . No. Explain.'

'I thought you wanted to go home.'

'Explain!'

'Would you like to see your home?'

'*See* it? It was destroyed!'

'It is discontinuous along the probability axis. Look!'

Something very strange and wonderful now swam into view in the rain. It was a huge, bluish-greenish globe, misty and cloud-covered, turning with majestic slowness against a black, starry background.

'Now you see it,' said the bird. 'Now you don't.'

A little less than two miles away, now, Arthur Dent stood still in his tracks. He could not believe what he could see, hanging there, shrouded in rain, but brilliant and vividly real against the night sky – the Earth. He gasped at the sight of it. Then, at the moment he gasped, it disappeared again. Then it appeared again. Then, and this was the bit that made him give up and stick straws in his hair, it turned into a sausage.

*

Random was also startled by the sight of this huge, blue and green and watery and misty sausage hanging above her. And now it was a string of sausages, or rather it was a string of sausages in which many of the sausages were missing. The whole brilliant string turned and span in a bewildering dance in the air and then gradually slowed, grew insubstantial and faded into the glistening darkness of the night.

'What was that?' asked Random, in a small voice.

'A glimpse along the probability axis of a discontinuously probable object.'

'I see.'

'Most objects mutate and change along their axis of probability, but the world of your origin does something slightly different. It lies on what you might call a fault line in the landscape of probability which means that at many probability coordinates the whole of it simply ceases to exist. It has an inherent instability, which is typical of anything that lies within what are usually designated the Plural sectors. Make sense?'

'No.'

'Want to go and see for yourself?'

'To . . . Earth?'

'Yes.'

'Is that possible?'

The bird *Guide* did not answer at once. It spread its wings and, with an easy grace, ascended into the air and flew out into the rain which, once again, was beginning to lighten.

It soared ecstatically up into the night sky, lights flashed around it, dimensions dithered in its wake. It swooped and turned and looped and turned again and came at last to rest two feet in front of Random's face, its wings beating slowly and silently.

It spoke to her again.

'Your universe is vast to you. Vast in time, vast in

space. That's because of the filters through which you perceive it. But I was built with no filters at all, which means I perceive the Mish Mash which contains all possible universes but which has, itself, no size at all. For me, anything is possible. I am omniscient and omnipotent, extremely vain, and, what is more, I come in a handy self-carrying package. You have to work out how much of the above is true.'

A slow smile spread over Random's face.

'You bloody little thing. You've been winding me up!'

'As I said, anything is possible.'

Random laughed. 'OK,' she said. 'Let's try and go to Earth. Let's go to Earth at some point on its, er . . .'

'Probability axis?'

'Yes. Where it hasn't been blown up. OK. So you're the *Guide*. How do we get a lift?'

'Reverse engineering.'

'What?'

'Reverse engineering. To me the flow of time is irrelevant. You decide what you want. I then merely make sure that it has already happened.'

'You're joking.'

'Anything is possible.'

Random frowned. 'You *are* joking, aren't you?'

'Let me put it another way,' said the bird. 'Reverse engineering enables us to shortcut all the business of waiting for one of the horribly few spaceships that passes through your galactic sector every year or so to make up its mind about whether or not it feels like giving you a lift. You want a lift, a ship arrives and gives you one. The pilot may think he has any one of a million reasons why he has decided to stop and pick you up. The real reason is that I have determined that he will.'

'This is you being extremely vain isn't it, little bird?'

The bird was silent.

'OK,' said Random. 'I want a ship to take me to Earth.'

'Will this one do?'

It was so silent that Random had not noticed the descending spaceship until it was nearly on top of her.

Arthur had noticed it. He was a mile away now and closing. Just after the illuminated sausage display had drawn to its conclusion he had noticed the faint glimmerings of further lights coming down out of the clouds and had, to begin with, assumed it to be another piece of flashy *son et lumière*.

It took a moment or so for it to dawn on him that it was an actual spaceship, and a moment or two longer for him to realize that it was dropping directly down to where he assumed his daughter to be. That was when, rain or no rain, leg injury or no leg injury, darkness or no darkness, he suddenly started really to run.

He fell almost immediately, slid and hurt his knee quite badly on a rock. He slithered back up to his feet and tried again. He had a horrible cold feeling that he was about to lose Random for ever. Limping and cursing, he ran. He didn't know what it was that had been in the box, but the name on it had been Ford Prefect, and that was the name he cursed as he ran.

The ship was one of the sexiest and most beautiful ones that Random had ever seen.

It was astounding. Silver, sleek, ineffable.

If she didn't know better she would have said it was an RW6. As it settled silently beside her she realized that it actually was an RW6 and she could scarcely breathe for excitement. An RW6 was the sort of thing you only saw in the sort of magazines that were designed to provoke civil unrest.

She was also extremely nervous. The manner and

timing of its arrival was deeply unsettling. Either it was the most bizarre coincidence or something very peculiar and worrying was going on. She waited a little tensely for the ship's hatch to open. Her *Guide* – she thought of it as hers now – was hovering lightly over her right shoulder, its wings barely fluttering.

The hatch opened. Just a little dim light escaped. A moment or two passed and a figure emerged. He stood still for a moment or so, obviously trying to accustom his eyes to the darkness. Then he caught sight of Random standing there, and seemed a little surprised. He started to walk towards her. Then suddenly he shouted in surprise and started to run at her.

Random was not a good person to take a run at on a dark night when she was feeling a little strung out. She had unconsciously been fingering the rock in her pocket from the moment she saw the craft coming down.

Still running, slithering, hurtling, bumping into trees, Arthur saw at last that he was too late. The ship had only been on the ground for about three minutes, and now, silently, gracefully, it was rising up above the trees again, turning smoothly in the fine speckle of rain to which the storm had now abated, climbing, climbing, tipping up its nose and, suddenly, effortlessly, hurtling up through the clouds.

Gone. Random was in it. It was impossible for Arthur to know this, but he just went ahead and knew it anyway. She was gone. He had had his stint at being a parent and could scarcely believe how badly he had done at it. He tried to continue running, but his feet were dragging, his knee was hurting like fury and he knew that he was too late.

He could not conceive that he could feel more wretched and awful than this, but he was wrong.

He limped his way at last to the cave where Random

had sheltered and opened the box. The ground bore the indentations of the spacecraft that had landed there only minutes before, but of Random there was no sign. He wandered disconsolately into the cave, found the empty box and piles of missing matter pellets strewn around the place. He felt a little cross about that. He'd tried to teach her about cleaning up after herself. Feeling a bit cross with her about something like that helped him feel less desolate about her leaving. He knew he had no means of finding her.

His foot knocked against something unexpected. He bent down to pick it up, and was thoroughly surprised to discover what it was. It was his old *Hitchhiker's Guide to the Galaxy*. How did that come to be in the cave? He had never returned to collect it from the scene of the crash. He had not wanted to revisit the crash and he had not wanted the *Guide* again. He had reckoned he was here on Lamuella, making sandwiches for good. How did it come to be in the cave? It was active. The words on the cover flashed DON'T PANIC at him.

He went out of the cave again into the dim and damp moonlight. He sat on a rock to have a look through the old *Guide*, and then discovered it wasn't a rock, it was a person.

18

Arthur leapt to his feet with a start of fear. It would be hard to say which he was more frightened of: that he might have hurt the person he had inadvertently sat on or that the person he had inadvertently sat on would hurt him back.

There seemed, on inspection, to be little immediate

cause for alarm on the second count. Whoever it was he had sat on was unconscious. That would probably go a great deal of the way towards explaining what he was doing lying there. He seemed to be breathing OK, though. Arthur felt his pulse. That was OK as well.

He was lying on his side, half curled up. It was so long ago and far away when Arthur had last done first aid that he really couldn't remember what it was he was supposed to do. The first thing he was supposed to do, he remembered, was to have a first aid kit about his person. Damn.

Should he roll him on to his back or not? Suppose he had any broken bones? Suppose he swallowed his tongue? Suppose he sued him? Who, apart from anything else, was he?

At that moment the unconscious man groaned loudly and rolled himself over.

Arthur wondered if he should—

He looked at him.

He looked at him again.

He looked at him again, just to make absolutely sure.

Despite the fact that he had been thinking he was feeling about as low as he possibly could, he experienced a terrible sinking feeling.

The figure groaned again and slowly opened his eyes. It took him a while to focus, then he blinked and stiffened.

'You!' said Ford Prefect.

'You!' said Arthur Dent.

Ford groaned again.

'What do you need to have explained this time?' he said, and closed his eyes in some kind of despair.

Five minutes later he was sitting up and rubbing the side of his head, where he had quite a large swelling.

'Who the hell was that woman?' he said. 'Why are we surrounded by squirrels, and what do they want?'

'I've been pestered by squirrels all night,' said Arthur. 'They keep on trying to give me magazines and stuff.'

Ford frowned. 'Really?' he said.

'And bits of rag.'

Ford thought.

'Oh,' he said. 'Is this near where your ship crashed?'

'Yes,' said Arthur. He said it a little tightly.

'That's probably it. Can happen. Ship's cabin robots get destroyed. The cyberminds that control them survive and start infesting the local wildlife. Can turn a whole ecosystem into some kind of helpless thrashing service industry, handing out hot towels and drinks to passers-by. Should be a law against it. Probably is. Probably also a law against there being a law against it so everybody can get nice and worked up. Hey ho. What did you say?'

'I said, and the woman is my daughter.'

Ford stopped rubbing his head.

'Say that one more time.'

'I said,' said Arthur huffily, 'the woman is my daughter.'

'I didn't know,' said Ford, 'that you had a daughter.'

'Well, there's probably a lot you don't know about me,' said Arthur. 'Come to mention it, there's probably a lot I don't know about me either.'

'Well, well, well. When did this happen, then?'

'I'm not quite sure.'

'That sounds like more familiar territory,' said Ford. 'Is there a mother involved?'

'Trillian.'

'*Trillian?* I didn't think that . . .'

'No. Look, it's a bit embarrassing.'

'I remember she told me once she had a kid but only,

sort of, in passing. I'm in touch with her from time to time. Never seen her with the kid.'

Arthur said nothing.

Ford started to feel the side of his head again in some bemusement.

'Are you *sure* this was *your* daughter?' he said.

'Tell me what happened.'

'Phroo. Long story. I was coming to pick up this parcel I'd sent to myself here care of you . . .'

'Well, what was that all about?'

'I think it may be something unimaginably dangerous.'

'And you sent it to *me*?' protested Arthur.

'Safest place I could think of. I thought I could rely on you to be absolutely boring and not open it. Anyway, coming in at night I couldn't find this village place. I was going by pretty basic information. I couldn't find any signal of any kind. I guess you don't have signals and stuff here.'

'That's what I like about it.'

'Then I did pick up a faint signal from your old copy of the *Guide*, so I homed in on that, thinking that would take me to you. I found I'd landed in some kind of wood. Couldn't figure out what was going on. I get out, and then see this woman standing there. I go up to say hello, then suddenly I see that she's got this thing!'

'What thing?'

'The thing I sent you! The new *Guide*! The bird thing! You were meant to keep it safe, you idiot, but this woman had the thing right there by her shoulder. I ran forward and she hit me with a rock.'

'I see,' said Arthur. 'What did you do?'

'Well, I fell over, of course. I was very badly hurt. She and the bird started to make off towards my ship. And when I say my ship, I mean an RW6.'

'A what?'

'An RW6, for Zark's sake. I've got this great relationship going now between my credit card and the *Guide*'s central computer. You would not believe that ship, Arthur, it's . . .'

'So an RW6 is a spaceship, then?'

'*Yes!* It's – oh, never mind. Look, just get some kind of grip will you, Arthur? Or at least get some kind of catalogue. At this point I was very worried. And, I think, semi-concussed. I was down on my knees and bleeding profusely, so I did the only thing I could think of, which was to beg. I said, please, for Zark's sake don't take my ship. And don't leave me stranded in the middle of some primitive Zarking forest with no medical help and a head injury. I could be in serious trouble and so could she.'

'What did she say?'

'She hit me on the head with the rock again.'

'I think I can confirm that that was my daughter.'

'Sweet kid.'

'You have to get to know her,' said Arthur.

'She eases up, does she?'

'No,' said Arthur, 'but you get a better sense of when to duck.'

Ford held his head and tried to see straight.

The sky was beginning to lighten in the west, which was where the sun rose. Arthur didn't particularly want to see it. The last thing he wanted after a hellish night like this one was some blasted day coming along and barging about the place.

'What are you doing in a place like this, Arthur?' demanded Ford.

'Well,' said Arthur, 'making sandwiches mostly.'

'What?'

'I am, probably was, the sandwich maker for a small tribe. It was a bit embarrassing really. When I first arrived, that is, when they rescued me from the wreckage of this super high-technology spacecraft which had crashed on their planet, they were very nice to me and I thought I should help them out a bit. You know, I'm an educated chap from a high-technology culture, I could show them a thing or two. And of course I couldn't. I haven't got the faintest idea, when it comes down to it, of how anything actually works. I don't mean like video-recorders, nobody knows how to work those. I mean just something like a pen or an artesian well or something. Not the foggiest. I couldn't help at all. One day I got glum and made myself a sandwich. That suddenly got them all excited. They'd never seen one before. It was just an idea that had never occurred to them, and I happen to quite like making sandwiches, so it all sort of developed from there.'

'And you *enjoyed* that?'

'Well, yes, I think I sort of did, really. Getting a good set of knives, that sort of thing.'

'You didn't, for instance, find it mind-witheringly, explosively, astoundingly, blisteringly dull?'

'Well, er, no. Not as such. Not actually blisteringly.'

'Odd. I would.'

'Well, I suppose we have a different outlook.'

'Yes.'

'Like the pikka birds.'

Ford had no idea what he was talking about and couldn't be bothered to ask. Instead he said, 'So how the hell do we get out of this place?'

'Well, I think the simplest way from here is just to follow the way down the valley to the plains, probably take an hour, and then walk round from there. I don't think I could face going back up and over the way I came.'

'Walk round *where* from there?'

'Well, back to the village. I suppose.' Arthur sighed a little forlornly.

'I don't want to go to any blasted village!' snapped Ford. 'We've got to get out of here!'

'Where? How?'

'I don't know, you tell me. You live here! There must be some way off this Zarking planet.'

'I don't know. What do you usually do? Sit around and wait for a passing spacecraft, I suppose.'

'Oh yes? And how many spacecraft have visited this Zarkforsaken little fleapit recently?'

'Well, a few years ago there was mine that crashed here by mistake. Then there was, er, Trillian, then the parcel delivery, and now you, and . . .'

'Yes, but *apart* from the usual suspects?'

'Well, er, I think pretty much none, so far as I know. Pretty quiet round here.'

As if deliberately to prove him wrong, there was a long, low distant roll of thunder.

Ford leapt to his feet fretfully and started pacing backwards and forwards in the feeble, painful light of the early dawn which lay streaked against the sky as if someone had dragged a piece of liver across it.

'You don't understand how important this is,' he said.

'What? You mean my daughter out there all alone in the Galaxy? You think I don't—'

'Can we feel sorry for the Galaxy later?' said Ford. 'This is very, very serious indeed. The *Guide* has been taken over. It's been bought out.'

Arthur leapt up. 'Oh very serious,' he shouted. 'Please fill me in straight away on some corporate publishing politics! I can't tell you how much it's been on my mind of late!'

'You don't understand! There's a whole new *Guide*!'

'Oh!' shouted Arthur again. 'Oh! Oh! Oh! I'm incoherent with excitement! I can hardly wait for it to come out to find out which are the most exciting spaceports to get bored hanging about in in some globular cluster I've never heard of. Please, can we rush to a store that's got it right this very instant?'

Ford narrowed his eyes.

'This is that thing you call sarcasm, isn't it?'

'Do you know,' bellowed Arthur, 'I think it is. I really think it might just be a crazy little thing called sarcasm seeping in at the edges of my manner of speech! Ford, I have had a *fucking* bad night! Will you please try and take that into account while you consider what fascinating bits of *badger-sputumly* inconsequential trivia to assail me with next?'

'Try to rest,' said Ford. 'I need to think.'

'Why do you need to *think*? Can't we just sit and go budumbudumbudum with our lips for a bit? Couldn't we just dribble gently and loll a little bit to the left for a few minutes? I can't stand it, Ford! I can't stand all this thinking and trying to work things out any more. You may think that I am just standing here barking . . .'

'Hadn't occurred to me, in fact.'

'. . . but I mean it! What is the point? We assume that every time we do anything we know what the consequences will be, i.e., more or less what we intend them to be. This is not only not always correct. It is wildly, crazily, stupidly cross-eyed-blithering-insectly wrong!'

'Which is exactly my point.'

'Thank you,' said Arthur, sitting down again. 'What?'

'Temporal reverse engineering.'

Arthur put his head in his hands and shook it gently from side to side.

'Is there any humane way,' he moaned, 'in which I can prevent you from telling me what temporary reverse bloody-whatsiting is?'

'No,' said Ford, 'because your daughter is caught up in the middle of it and it is deadly, deadly serious.'

Thunder rolled in the pause.

'All right,' said Arthur. 'Tell me.'

'I leaped out of a high-rise office window.'

This cheered Arthur up.

'Oh!' he said. 'Why don't you do it again?'

'I did.'

'Hmmm,' said Arthur, disappointed. 'Obviously no good came of it.'

'The first time I managed to save myself by the most astonishing and – I say this in all modesty – fabulous piece of ingenious quick-thinking, agility, fancy footwork and self-sacrifice.'

'What was the self-sacrifice?'

'I jettisoned half of a much loved and I think irreplaceable pair of shoes.'

'Why was that self-sacrifice?'

'Because they were mine!' said Ford crossly.

'I think we have different value systems.'

'Well, mine's better.'

'That's according to your ... oh never mind. So having saved yourself very cleverly once you very sensibly went and jumped again. Please don't tell me why. Just tell me what happened if you must.'

'I fell straight into the open cockpit of a passing jet towncar whose pilot had just accidentally pushed the eject button when he meant only to change tracks on the stereo. Now, even I couldn't think that that was particularly clever of me.'

'Oh, I don't know,' said Arthur wearily. 'I expect you probably sneaked into his jetcar the previous night and set the pilot's least favourite track to play or something.'

'No, I didn't,' said Ford.

'Just checking.'

'Though oddly enough, *somebody else did*. And this is the nub. You could trace the chain and branches of crucial events and coincidences back and back. Turned out the new *Guide* had done it. That bird.'

'What bird?'

'You haven't seen it?'

'No.'

'Oh. It's a lethal little thing. Looks pretty, talks big, collapses waveforms selectively at will.'

'What does that mean?'

'Temporal reverse engineering.'

'Oh,' said Arthur. 'Oh yes.'

'The question is, *who is it really doing it for*?'

'I've actually got a sandwich in my pocket,' said Arthur, delving. 'Would you like a bit?'

'Yeah, OK.'

'It's a bit squished and sodden, I'm afraid.'

'Never mind.'

They munched for a bit.

'It's quite good, in fact,' said Ford. 'What's the meat in it?'

'Perfectly Normal Beast.'

'Not come across that one. So, the question is,' Ford continued, 'who is the bird really doing it for? What's the real game here?'

'Mmm,' ate Arthur.

'When I found the bird,' continued Ford, 'which I did by a series of coincidences that are interesting in themselves, it put on the most fantastic multi-dimensional display of pyrotechnics I've ever seen. It then said that it would put its services at my disposal in my universe. I said, thanks but no thanks. It said that it would anyway, whether I liked it or not. I said just try it, and it said it would and, indeed, already had done. I said we'd see about that and it said that we would. That's when I decided to pack the thing up and get it out of there. So I sent it to you for safety.'

'Oh yes? Whose?'

'Never you mind. Then, what with one thing and another, I thought it prudent to jump out of the window again, being fresh out of other options at the time. Luckily for me the jetcar was there otherwise I would have had to fall back on ingenious quick-thinking, agility, maybe another shoe or, failing all else, the ground. But it meant that, whether I liked it or not, the *Guide* was, well, working for me, and that was deeply worrying.'

'Why?'

'Because if you've got the *Guide* you think that you are the one it's working for. Everything went swimmingly smoothly for me from then on, up to the very moment that I come up against the totty with the rock, then, bang, I'm history. I'm out of the loop.'

'Are you referring to my daughter?'

'As politely as I can. She's the next one in the chain who will think that everything is going fabulously for her. She can beat whoever she likes around the head with bits of the landscape, everything will just swim for her until she's done whatever she's supposed to do and then it will be all up for her too. It's reverse temporal engineering, and clearly nobody understood what was being unleashed!'

'Like me, for instance.'

'What? Oh, wake up, Arthur. Look, let me try it again. The new *Guide* came out of the research labs. It made use of this new technology of Unfiltered Perception. Do you know what that means?'

'Look, I've been making sandwiches, for Bob's sake!'

'Who's Bob?'

'Never mind. Just carry on.'

'Unfiltered Perception means it perceives everything. Got that? *I* don't perceive everything. *You* don't perceive everything. We have filters. The new *Guide* doesn't have any sense filters. It perceives *everything*. It wasn't a complicated technological idea. It was just a question of leaving a bit out. Got it?'

'Why don't I just say that I've got it, and then you can carry on regardless.'

'Right. Now because the bird can perceive every possible Universe, it is present in every possible universe. Yes?'

'Y . . . e . . . e . . . s. Ish.'

'So what happens is, the bozos in the marketing and accounting departments say, oh that sounds good, doesn't that mean we only have to make one of them and then sell it an infinite number of times? Don't squint at me like that, Arthur, this is how accountants *think*!'

'That's quite clever, isn't it?'

'No! It is fantastically *stupid*. Look. The machine's only a little *Guide*. It's got some quite clever cybertechnology in it, but because it has Unfiltered Perception, any smallest move it makes has the power of a virus. It can propagate throughout space, time and a million other dimensions. Anything can be focused anywhere in any of the universes that you and I move in. Its power is recursive. Think of a computer program. Somewhere, there is one key instruction, and everything else is just functions calling themselves, or brackets billowing out endlessly through an infinite address space. What happens when the brackets collapse? Where's the final "end if"? Is any of this making sense? Arthur?'

'Sorry, I was nodding off for a moment. Something about the Universe, yes?'

'Something about the Universe, yes,' said Ford, wearily. He sat down again.

'All right,' he said. 'Think about this. You know who I think I saw at the *Guide* offices? Vogons. Ah, I see I've said a word you understand at last.'

Arthur leapt to his feet.

'That noise,' he said.

'What noise?'

'The thunder.'

'What about it?'

'It isn't thunder. It's the spring migration of the Perfectly Normal Beasts. It's started.'

'What are these animals you keep on about?'

'I don't keep on about them. I just put bits of them in sandwiches.'

'Why are they called Perfectly Normal Beasts?'

Arthur told him.

It wasn't often that Arthur had the pleasure of seeing Ford's eyes open wide with astonishment.

19

It was a sight that Arthur never quite got used to, or tired of. He and Ford had tracked their way swiftly along the side of the small river that flowed down along the bed of the valley, and when at last they reached the margin of the plains they pulled themselves up into the branches of a large tree to get a better view of one of the stranger and more wonderful visions that the Galaxy has to offer.

The great thunderous herd of thousands upon thousands of Perfectly Normal Beasts was sweeping in magnificent array across the Anhondo Plain. In the early pale light of the morning, as the great animals charged through the fine steam of the sweat of their bodies mingled with the muddy mist churned up by their pounding hooves, their appearance seemed a little unreal and ghostly anyway, but what was heart-stopping about them was where they came from and where they went to, which appeared to be, simply, nowhere.

They formed a solid, charging phalanx roughly a

hundred yards wide and half a mile long. The phalanx never moved, except that it exhibited a slight gradual drift sideways and backwards for the eight or nine days that it regularly appeared for. But though the phalanx stayed more or less constant, the great beasts of which it was composed charged steadily at upwards of twenty miles an hour, appearing suddenly from thin air at one end of the plain, and disappearing equally abruptly at the other end.

No one knew where they came from, no one knew where they went. They were so important to the lives of the Lamuellans, it was almost as if nobody liked to ask. Old Thrashbarg had said on one occasion that sometimes if you received an answer, the question might be taken away. Some of the villagers had privately said that this was the only properly wise thing they'd ever heard Thrashbarg say, and after a short debate on the matter, had put it down to chance.

The noise of the pounding of the hooves was so intense that it was hard to hear anything else above it.

'What did you say?' shouted Arthur.

'I said,' shouted Ford, 'this looks like it might be some kind of evidence of dimensional drift.'

'Which is what?' shouted Arthur back.

'Well, a lot of people are beginning to worry that space–time is showing signs of cracking up with everything that's happening to it. There are quite a lot of worlds where you can see how the landmasses have cracked up and moved around just from the weirdly long or meandering routes that migrating animals take. This might be something like that. We live in twisted times. Still, in the absence of a decent spaceport . . .'

Arthur looked at him in a kind of frozen way.

'What do you mean?' he said.

'What do you mean, what do I mean?' shouted Ford.

'You know perfectly well what I mean. We're going to ride our way out of here.'

'Are you seriously suggesting we try to ride a Perfectly Normal Beast?'

'Yeah. See where it goes to.'

'We'll be killed! No,' said Arthur, suddenly. 'We won't be killed. At least I won't. Ford, have you ever heard of a planet called Stavromula Beta?'

Ford frowned. 'Don't think so,' he said. He pulled out his own battered old copy of *The Hitchhiker's Guide to the Galaxy* and accessed it. 'Any funny spelling?' he said.

'Don't know. I've only ever heard it said, and that was by someone who had a mouthful of other people's teeth. You remember I told you about Agrajag?'

Ford thought for a moment. 'You mean the guy who was convinced you were getting him killed over and over again?'

'Yes. One of the places he claimed I'd got him killed was Stavromula Beta. Someone tries to shoot me, it seems. I duck and Agrajag, or at least, one of his many reincarnations, gets hit. It seems that this has definitely happened at some point in time so, I suppose, I can't get killed at least until after I've ducked on Stavromula Beta. Only no one's ever heard of it.'

'Hmm.' Ford tried a few other searches of the *Hitchhiker's Guide*, but drew a blank.

'Nothing,' he said.

'I was just . . . no, I've never heard of it,' said Ford finally. He wondered why it was ringing a very, very faint bell, though.

'OK,' said Arthur. 'I've seen the way the Lamuellan hunters trap Perfectly Normal Beasts. If you spear one in the herd it just gets trampled, so they have to lure them out one at a time for the kill. It's very like the way a matador works, you know, with a brightly coloured cape. You get one to charge at you and then step aside and execute a rather elegant swing through with the cape. Have you got anything like a brightly coloured cape about you?'

'This do?' said Ford, handing him his towel.

20

Leaping on to the back of a one-and-a-half-ton Perfectly Normal Beast migrating through your world at a thundering thirty miles an hour is not as easy as it might at first seem. Certainly it is not as easy as the Lamuellan hunters made it seem, and Arthur Dent was prepared to discover that this might turn out to be the difficult bit.

What he hadn't been prepared to discover, however, was how difficult it was even *getting* to the difficult bit. It was the bit that was supposed to be the easy bit which turned out to be practically impossible.

They couldn't even catch the attention of a single animal. The Perfectly Normal Beasts were so intent on working up a good thunder with their hooves, heads down, shoulders forward, back legs pounding the ground into porridge that it would have taken something not merely startling but actually geological to disturb them.

The sheer amount of thundering and pounding was, in the end, more than Arthur and Ford could deal with. After they had spent nearly two hours prancing about doing increasingly foolish things with a medium-sized floral patterned bath towel, they had not managed to get even one of the great beasts thundering and pounding past them to do so much as glance casually in their direction.

They were within three feet of the horizontal avalanche of sweating bodies. To have been much nearer would have been to risk instant death, chrono-logic or no chrono-logic. Arthur had seen what remained of any Perfectly Normal Beast which, as the result of a clumsy mis-throw by a young and inexperienced Lamuellan hunter, got speared while still thundering and pounding with the herd.

One stumble was all it took. No prior appointment with death on Stavromula Beta, wherever the hell Stavromula Beta was, would save you or anybody else from the thunderous, mangling pounding of those hooves.

At last, Arthur and Ford staggered back. They sat down, exhausted and defeated, and started to criticize each other's technique with the towel.

'You've got to flick it more,' complained Ford. 'You need more follow-through from the elbow if you're going to get those blasted creatures to notice anything at all.'

'Follow-through?' protested Arthur. *'You* need more suppleness in the wrist.'

'You need more after-flourish,' countered Ford.

'You need a bigger towel.'

'You need,' said another voice, 'a pikka bird.'

'You what?'

The voice had come from behind them. They turned, and there, standing behind them in the early morning sun, was Old Thrashbarg.

'To attract the attention of a Perfectly Normal Beast,' he said, as he walked forward towards them, 'you need a pikka bird. Like this.'

From under the rough, cassocky robe-like thing he wore he drew a small pikka bird. It sat restlessly on Old

Thrashbarg's hand and peered intently at Bob knows what darting around about three feet six inches in front of it.

Ford instantly went into the sort of alert crouch he liked to do when he wasn't quite sure what was going on or what he ought to do about it. He waved his arms around very slowly in what he hoped was an ominous manner.

'Who is this?' he hissed.

'It's just Old Thrashbarg,' said Arthur quietly. 'And I wouldn't bother with all the fancy movements. He's just as experienced a bluffer as you are. You could end up dancing around each other all day.'

'The bird,' hissed Ford again. 'What's the bird?'

'It's just a bird!' said Arthur impatiently. 'It's like any other bird. It lays eggs and goes *ark* at things you can't see. Or *kar* or *rit* or something.'

'Have you *seen* one lay eggs?' said Ford, suspiciously.

'For Heaven's sake, of course I have,' said Arthur. 'And I've eaten hundreds of them. Make rather a good omelette. The secret is little cubes of cold butter and then whipping it lightly with . . .'

'I don't want a Zarking recipe,' said Ford. 'I just want to be sure it's a real bird and not some kind of multi-dimensional cybernightmare.'

He slowly stood up from his crouched position and started to brush himself down. He was still watching the bird, though.

'So,' said Old Thrashbarg to Arthur. 'Is it written that Bob shall once more take back unto himself the benediction of his once-given Sandwich Maker?'

Ford almost went back into his crouch.

'It's all right,' muttered Arthur, 'he always talks like that.' Aloud, he said, 'Ah, venerable Thrashbarg. Um, yes. I'm afraid I think I'm going to have to be popping off now. But young Drimple, my apprentice, will be a fine sandwich maker in my stead. He has the aptitude, a deep love of sandwiches, and the skills he has acquired so far, though rudimentary as yet, will, in time mature and, er, well, I think he'll work out OK is what I'm trying to say.'

Old Thrashbarg regarded him gravely. His old grey eyes moved sadly. He held his arms aloft, one still carrying a bobbing pikka bird, the other his staff.

'O Sandwich Maker from Bob!' he pronounced. He paused, furrowed his brow, and sighed as he closed his eyes in pious contemplation. 'Life,' he said, 'will be a very great deal less weird without you!'

Arthur was stunned.

'Do you know,' he said, 'I think that's the nicest thing anybody's ever said to me.'

'Can we get on, please?' said Ford.

Something was already happening. The presence of the pikka bird at the end of Thrashbarg's outstretched arm was sending tremors of interest through the thundering herd. The odd head flicked momentarily in their direction. Arthur began to remember some of the Perfectly Normal Beast hunts he had witnessed. He recalled that as well as the hunter-matadors brandishing their capes there were always others standing behind them holding pikka birds. He had always assumed that, like him, they had just come along to watch.

Old Thrashbarg moved forward, a little closer to the rolling herd. Some of the Beasts were now tossing their heads back with interest at the sight of the pikka bird.

Old Thrashbarg's outstretched arms were trembling.

Only the pikka bird itself seemed to show no interest in what was going on. A few anonymous molecules of air nowhere in particular engaged all of its perky attention.

'Now!' exclaimed Old Thrashbarg at last. 'Now you may work them with the towel!'

Arthur advanced with Ford's towel, moving the way the hunter-matadors did, with a kind of elegant strut that did not come at all naturally to him. But now he knew what to do and that it was right. He brandished and flicked the towel a few times, to be ready for the moment, and then he watched.

Some distance away he spotted the Beast he wanted. Head down, it was galloping towards him, right on the very edge of the herd. Old Thrashbarg twitched the bird, the Beast looked up, tossed its head, and then, just as its head was coming down again, Arthur flourished the towel in the Beast's line of sight. It tossed its head again in bemusement, and its eyes followed the movement of the towel.

He had got the Beast's attention.

From that moment on, it seemed the most natural thing to coax and draw the animal towards him. Its head was up, cocked slightly to one side. It was slowing to a canter and then a trot. A few seconds later the huge thing was standing there amongst them, snorting, panting, sweating, and sniffing excitedly at the pikka bird, which appeared not to have noticed its arrival at all. With strange sort of sweeping movements of his arms Old Thrashbarg kept the pikka bird in front of the Beast, but always out of its reach and always downwards. With strange sort of sweeping movements of the towel, Arthur kept drawing the Beast's attention this way and that – always downwards.

'I don't think I've ever seen anything quite so stupid in my life,' muttered Ford to himself.

At last, the Beast dropped, bemused but docile, to its knees.

'Go!' whispered Old Thrashbarg urgently, to Ford. 'Go! Go now!'

Ford leapt up on to the great creature's back, scrabbling amongst its thick knotty fur for purchase, grasping great handfuls of the stuff to hold him steady once he was in position.

'Now, Sandwich Maker! Go!' He performed some elaborate sign and ritual handshake which Arthur couldn't quite get the hang of because Old Thrashbarg had obviously made it up on the spur of the moment, then he pushed Arthur forward. Taking a deep breath, he clambered up behind Ford on to the great, hot, heaving back of the beast and held on tight. Huge muscles the size of sea lions rippled and flexed beneath him.

Old Thrashbarg held the bird suddenly aloft. The Beast's head swivelled up to follow it. Thrashbarg pushed upwards and upwards repeatedly with his arms and with the pikka bird; and slowly, heavily the Perfectly Normal Beast lurched up off its knees and stood, at last, swaying slightly. Its two riders held on fiercely and nervously.

Arthur gazed out over the sea of hurtling animals, straining in an attempt to see where it was they were going, but there was nothing but heat haze.

'Can you see anything?' he said to Ford.

'No.' Ford twisted round to glance back, trying to see if there was any clue as to where they had come from. Still, nothing.

Arthur shouted down at Thrashbarg.

'Do you know where they come from?' he called. 'Or where they're going?'

'The domain of the King!' shouted Old Thrashbarg back.

'King?' shouted Arthur in surprise. 'What King?' The Perfectly Normal Beast was swaying and rocking restlessly under him.

'What do you mean, *what* King?' shouted Old Thrashbarg. '*The* King.'

'It's just that you never mentioned a King,' shouted Arthur back, in some consternation.

'What?' shouted Old Thrashbarg. The thrumming of a thousand hooves was very hard to hear over, and the old man was concentrating on what he was doing.

Still holding the bird aloft, he led the Beast slowly round till it was once more parallel with the motion of its great herd. He moved forward. The Beast followed. He moved forward again. The Beast followed again. At last, the Beast was lumbering forward with a little momentum.

'I said you never mentioned a King!' shouted Arthur again.

'I didn't say *a* King,' shouted Old Thrashbarg, 'I said the King.'

He drew back his arm and then hurled it forward with all his strength, casting the pikka bird up into the air above the herd. This seemed to catch the pikka bird completely by surprise as it had obviously not been paying any attention at all to what was going on. It took it a moment or two to work out what was happening, then it unfurled its little wings, spread them out, and flew.

'Go!' shouted Thrashbarg. 'Go and meet your destiny, Sandwich Maker!'

Arthur wasn't so sure about wanting to meet his destiny as such. He just wanted to get to wherever it was they were going so he could get back off this creature again. He didn't feel at all safe up there. The Beast was gathering speed as it followed in the wake of the pikka bird. And then it was in at the fringes of the great tide of animals, and in a moment or two, with its head down, the pikka bird forgotten, it was running with the herd again and rapidly approaching the point at which the herd was vanishing into thin air. Arthur and Ford held on to the great monster for dear life, surrounded on all sides by hurtling mountains of bodies.

'Go! Ride that Beast!' shouted Thrashbarg. His distant

voice reverberated faintly in their ears. 'Ride that Perfectly Normal Beast! Ride it, ride it!'

Ford shouted in Arthur's ear, 'Where did he say we were going?'

'He said something about a King,' shouted Arthur in return, holding on desperately.

'What King?'

'That's what I said. He just said *the* King.'

'I didn't know there was a *the* King,' shouted Ford.

'Nor did I,' shouted Arthur back.

'Except of course for *the* King,' shouted Ford. 'And I don't suppose he meant him.'

'*What* King?' shouted Arthur.

The point of exit was almost upon them. Just ahead of them, Perfectly Normal Beasts were galloping into nothingness and vanishing.

'What do you mean, *what* King?' shouted Ford. '*I* don't know what King. I'm only saying that he couldn't possibly mean *the* King, so I don't know what he means.'

'Ford, I don't know what you're talking about.'

'So?' said Ford. Then with a sudden rush, the stars came on, turned and twisted around their heads, and then, just as suddenly, turned off again.

21

Misty grey buildings loomed and flickered. They bounced up and down in a highly embarrassing way.

What sort of buildings were they?

What were they for? What did they remind her of?

It's so difficult to know what things are supposed to be when you suddenly turn up unexpectedly on a different world which has a different culture, a different set of the most basic assumptions about life, and also incredibly dull and meaningless architecture.

The sky above the buildings was a cold and hostile black. The stars, which should have been blindingly brilliant points of light this far from the sun, were blurred and dulled by the thickness of the huge shielding bubble. Perspex or something like it. Something dull and heavy anyway.

Tricia wound the tape back again to the beginning.

She knew there was something slightly odd about it.

Well, in fact, there were about a million things that were slightly odd about it, but there was one that was nagging at her and she hadn't quite got it.

She sighed and yawned.

As she waited for the tape to rewind she cleared away some of the dirty polystyrene coffee cups that had accumulated on the editing desk and tipped them into the bin.

She was sitting in a small editing suite at a video production company in Soho. She had 'Do not disturb' notices plastered all over the door, and a block on all incoming calls at the switchboard. This was originally to protect her astonishing scoop, but now it was to protect her from embarrassment.

She would watch the tape all the way through again from the beginning. If she could bear to. She might do some fast-forwarding here and there.

It was about four o'clock on Monday afternoon, and she had a kind of sick feeling. She was trying to work out what the cause of this slightly sick feeling was, and there was no shortage of candidates.

First of all, it had all come on top of the overnight flight from New York. The red eye. Always a killer, that.

Then being accosted by aliens on her lawn and flown to the planet Rupert. She was not sufficiently experienced in that sort of thing to be able to say for sure that that was always a killer, but she would be prepared to bet that those who went through it regularly cursed it. There were always stress charts being published in magazines. Fifty stress points for losing your job. Seventy-five points for a divorce or changing your hairstyle and so on. None of them ever mentioned being accosted on your lawn by aliens and then being flown to the planet Rupert, but she was sure it was worth a few dozen points.

It wasn't that the journey had been particularly stressful. It had been extremely dull, in fact. Certainly it had been no more stressful than the trip she had just taken across the Atlantic and it had taken roughly the same time, about seven hours.

Well, that was pretty astounding wasn't it? Flying to the outer limits of the solar system in the same time that it took to fly to New York meant they must have some fantastic unheard-of form of propulsion in the ship. She quizzed her hosts about it and they agreed that it was pretty good.

'But how does it *work*?' she had demanded excitedly. She was still quite excited at the beginning of the trip.

She found that part of the tape and played it through to herself. The Grebulons, which is what they called themselves, were politely showing her which buttons they pressed to make the ship go.

'Yes, but what *principle* does it work on?' she heard herself demand, from behind the camera.

'Oh, you mean is it something like a warp drive or something like that?' they said.

'Yes,' persisted Tricia. 'What *is* it?'

'It probably is something of the kind,' they said.

'Like *what*?'

'Warp drive, photon drive, something like that. You'd have to ask the Flight Engineer.'

'Which one is he?'

'We don't know. We have all lost our minds, you see.'

'Oh yes,' said Tricia, a little faintly. 'So you said. Um, how did you lose your minds, exactly, then?'

'We don't know,' they said, patiently.

'Because you've lost your minds,' echoed Tricia, glumly.

'Would you like to watch television? It is a long flight. We watch television. It is something we enjoy.'

All of this riveting stuff was on the tape, and fine viewing it made. First of all the picture quality was extremely poor. Tricia didn't know why this was, exactly. She had a feeling that the Grebulons responded to a slightly different range of light frequencies, and that there had been a lot of ultra-violet around which was mucking up the video camera. There were a lot of interference patterns and video snow as well. Probably something to do with the warp drive that none of them knew the first thing about.

So what she had on tape, essentially, was a bunch of slightly thin and discoloured people sitting around watching televisions that were showing network broadcasts. She had also pointed the camera out of the very tiny viewport near her seat and got a nice, slightly streaky effect of stars. She knew it was real, but it would have taken a good three or four minutes to fake.

In the end she had decided to save her precious videotape for Rupert itself and had simply sat back and watched television with them. She had even dozed off for a while.

So part of her sick feeling came from the sense that she had had all that time in an alien spacecraft of astounding technological design, and had spent most of it dozing in front of reruns of *M*A*S*H* and *Cagney and Lacey*. But what else was there to do? She had taken some photos as well, of course, all of which had subsequently turned out to be badly fogged when she got them back from the chemist.

Another part of her sick feeling probably came from the landing on Rupert. This at least had been dramatic and hair-raising. The ship had come sweeping in over a dark and sombre landscape, a terrain so desperately far removed from the heat and light of its parent sun that it seemed like a map of the psychological scars on the mind of an abandoned child.

Lights blazed through the frozen darkness and guided the ship into the mouth of some kind of cave that seemed to bend itself open to accept the small craft.

Unfortunately, because of the angle of their approach, and the depth at which the small thick viewport was set into the craft's skin, it hadn't been possible to get the video camera to point directly at any of it. She ran through that bit of the tape.

The camera was pointing directly at the sun.

This is normally very bad for a video camera. But when the sun is roughly a third of a billion miles away it doesn't do any harm. In fact it hardly makes any impression at all. You just get a small point of light right in the middle of the frame, which could be just about anything. It was just one star in a multitude.

Tricia fast-forwarded.

Ah. Now, the next bit had been quite promising. They had emerged out of the ship into a vast, grey, hangar-like structure. This was clearly alien technology on a dramatic scale. Huge grey buildings under the dark canopy of the Perspex bubble. These were the same buildings that she had been looking at at the end of the tape. She had taken more footage of them while leaving Rupert a few hours later, just as she was about to reboard the spacecraft for the journey home. What did they remind her of?

Well, as much as anything else they reminded her of a film set from just about any low-budget science-fiction movie of the last twenty years. A lot larger, of course, but it all looked thoroughly tawdry and unconvincing on the video screen. Apart from the dreadful picture quality she had been struggling with the unexpected effects of gravity that was appreciably lower than that on Earth, and she had found it very hard to keep the camera from bouncing around in an embarrassingly unprofessional way. It was therefore impossible to make out any detail.

And now here was the Leader coming forward to greet her, smiling and sticking his hand out.

That was all he was called. The Leader.

None of the Grebulons had names, largely because they couldn't think of any. Tricia discovered that some of them had thought of calling themselves after characters from television programmes they had picked up from Earth, but hard as they had tried to call each other Wayne and Bobby and Chuck, some remnant of something lurking deep in the cultural subconscious they had brought with them from the distant stars which were their homes must have told them that this really wasn't right and wouldn't do.

The Leader had looked pretty much like all the others. Possibly a bit less thin. He said how much he enjoyed her shows on TV, that he was her greatest fan, how glad he was that she had been able to come along and visit them on Rupert and how much everybody had been looking forward to her coming, how he hoped the flight had been comfortable and so on. There was no particular sense she could detect of being any kind of emissary from the stars or anything.

Certainly, watching it now on videotape, he just looked like some guy in costume and make-up, standing in front of a set that wouldn't hold up too well if you leant against it.

She sat staring at the screen with her face cradled in her hands, and shaking her head in slow bewilderment.

This was *awful*.

Not only was this bit awful but she knew what was coming next. It was the bit where the Leader asked if she was hungry after the flight, and would she perhaps like to come and have something to eat? They could discuss things over a little dinner.

She could remember what she was thinking at this point.

Alien food.

How was she going to deal with it?

Would she actually have to eat it? Would she have access to some sort of paper napkin she could spit stuff out into? Wouldn't there be all sorts of differential immunity problems?

It turned out to be hamburgers.

Not only did it turn out to be hamburgers, but the hamburgers it turned out to be were very clearly and obviously McDonald's hamburgers which had been reheated in a microwave. It wasn't just the look of them. It wasn't just the smell. It was the polystyrene clamshell packages they came in which had 'McDonald's' printed all over them.

'Eat! Enjoy!' said the Leader. 'Nothing is too good for our honoured guest!'

This was in his private apartment. Tricia had looked around it in bewilderment that had bordered on fear but had nevertheless got it all on videotape.

The apartment had a waterbed in it. And a midi hi-fi. And one of those tall electrically illuminated glass things which sit on table tops and appear to have large globules of sperm floating about in them. The walls were covered in velvet.

The leader lounged against a brown corduroy bean bag and squirted breath-freshener into his mouth.

Tricia began to feel very scared, suddenly. She was further from Earth than any human being, to her knowledge, had ever been, and she was with an alien creature, who was lounging against a brown corduroy bean bag and squirting breath-freshener into his mouth.

She didn't want to make any false moves. She didn't want to alarm him. But there were things she had to know.

'How did you ... where did you get ... this?' she asked, gesturing around the room, nervously.

'The decor?' asked the Leader. 'Do you like it? It is very sophisticated. We are a sophisticated people, we Grebulons. We buy sophisticated consumer durables ... by mail order.'

Tricia had nodded tremendously slowly at this point.

'Mail order ...' she had said.

The Leader chuckled. It was one of those dark chocolate reassuring silky chuckles.

'I think you think they ship it here. No! Ha Ha! We have arranged a special box number in New Hampshire. We make regular pick-up visits. Ha Ha!' He lounged back in a relaxed fashion on his bean bag, reached for a reheated french fry and nibbled the end of it, an amused smile playing across his lips.

Tricia could feel her brain beginning to bubble very slightly. She kept the video camera going.

'How do you, well, er, how do you pay for these wonderful ... things?'

The Leader chuckled again.

'American Express,' he said with a nonchalant shrug.

Tricia nodded slowly again. She knew that they gave cards exclusively to just about anybody.

'And these?' she said, holding up the hamburger he had presented her with.

'It is very easy,' said the Leader. 'We stand in line.'

Again, Tricia realized with a cold, trickling feeling going down her spine, that explained an awful lot.

She hit the fast-forward button again. There was nothing of any use here at all. It was all nightmarish madness. She could have faked something that would have looked more convincing.

Another sick feeling began to creep over her as she watched this hopeless awful tape, and she began, with slow horror, to realize that it must be the answer.

She must be . . .

She shook her head and tried to get a grip.

An overnight flight going east . . . The sleeping pills she had taken to get her through it. The vodka she'd had to set the sleeping pills going.

What else? Well. There was seventeen years of obsession that a glamorous man with two heads, one of which was disguised as a parrot in a cage, had tried to pick her up at a party but had then impatiently flown off to another planet in a flying saucer. There suddenly seemed to be all sorts of bothersome aspects to that idea that had never really occurred to her. Never occurred to her. In seventeen years.

She stuffed her fist into her mouth.

She must get help.

Then there had been Eric Bartlett banging on about alien spacecraft landing on her lawn. And before that . . . New York had been, well, very hot and stressful. The high hopes and the bitter disappointment. The astrology stuff.

She must have had a nervous breakdown.

That was it. She was exhausted and she had had a nervous breakdown and had started hallucinating some time after she got home. She had dreamt the whole story. An alien race of people dispossessed of their own lives and histories, stuck on a remote outpost of our solar system and filling their cultural vacuum with our cultural junk. Ha! It was nature's way of telling her to check into an expensive medical establishment very quickly.

She was very, very sick. She looked at how many large coffees she'd got through as well, and realized how heavily she was breathing and how fast.

Part of solving any problem, she told herself, was realizing that you had it. She started to bring her breathing under control. She had caught herself in time. She had seen where she was. She was on the way back from whatever psychological precipice she had been on the brink of. She started to calm down, to calm down, to calm down. She sat back in the chair and closed her eyes.

After a while, now that she was breathing normally again, she opened them again.

So where had she got this tape from, then?

It was still running.

All right. It was a fake.

She had faked it herself, that was it.

It must have been her who had faked it because her voice was all over the soundtrack, asking questions. Every now and then the camera would swing down at the end of a shot and she would see her own feet in her own shoes. She had faked it and she had no recollection of faking it or any idea of why she had done it.

Her breathing was getting hectic again as she watched the snowy, flickering screen.

She must *still* be hallucinating.

She shook her head, trying to make it go away. She had no memory of faking any of this very obviously fake stuff. On the other hand she did seem to have memories that were very *like* the faked stuff. She continued to watch in a bewildered trance.

The person she imagined to be called the Leader was questioning her about astrology and she was answering smoothly and calmly. Only she could detect the well-disguised rising panic in her own voice.

The Leader pushed a button, and a maroon velvet wall slid aside, revealing a large bank of flat TV monitors.

Each of the monitors was showing a kaleidoscope of different images: a few seconds from a game show, a few seconds from a cop show, a few seconds from a supermarket warehouse security system, a few seconds from somebody's holiday movies, a few seconds of sex, a few seconds of news, a few seconds of comedy. It was clear that the Leader was very proud of all this stuff and he was waving his hands like a conductor while continuing at the same time to talk complete gibberish.

Another wave of his hands, and all the screens cleared to form one giant computer screen showing in diagrammatic form all the planets of the solar system and mapped out against a background of the stars in their constellations. The display was completely static.

'We have great skills,' the Leader was saying. 'Great skills in computation, in cosmological trigonometry, in three-dimensional navigational calculus. Great skills. Great, great skills. Only we have lost them. It is too bad. We like to have skills only they have gone. They are in space somewhere, hurtling. With our names and the details of our homes and loved ones. Please,' he said, gesturing her forward to sit at the computer's console, 'be skilful for us.'

Obviously what happened next was that Tricia

quickly set the video camera up on its tripod to capture the whole scene. She then walked into shot herself and sat down calmly in front of the giant computer display, spent a few moments familiarizing herself with the interface and then started smoothly and competently to pretend that she had the faintest idea what she was doing.

It hadn't been that difficult, in fact.

She was, after all, a mathematician and astrophysicist by training and a television presenter by experience, and what science she had forgotten over the years she was more than capable of making up by bluffing.

The computer she was working on was clear evidence that the Grebulons came from a far more advanced and sophisticated culture than their current vacuous state suggested, and with its aid she was able, within about half an hour, to cobble together a rough working model of the solar system.

It wasn't particularly accurate or anything, but it looked good. The planets were whizzing around in reasonably good simulations of their orbits, and you could watch the movement of the whole piece of virtual cosmological clockwork from any point within the system – very roughly. You could watch from Earth, you could watch from Mars, etc. You could watch from the surface of the planet Rupert. Tricia had been quite impressed with herself, but also very impressed with the computer system she was working on. Using a computer workstation on Earth the task would probably have taken a year or so of programming.

When she was finished, the Leader came up behind her and watched. He was very pleased and delighted with what she had achieved.

'Good,' he said. 'And now, please, I would like you to demonstrate how to use the system you have just designed to translate the information in this book for me.'

Quietly he put a book down in front of her.

It was *You and Your Planets* by Gail Andrews.

Tricia stopped the tape again.

She was definitely feeling very wobbly indeed. The feeling that she was hallucinating had now receded, but had not left anything any easier or clearer in her head.

She pushed her seat back from the editing desk and wondered what to do. Years ago she had left the field of astronomical research because she knew, without any doubt whatsoever, that she had met a being from another planet. At a party. And she had also known, without any doubt whatsoever, that she would have made herself a laughing stock if she had ever said so. But how could she study cosmology and *not* say anything about the single most important thing she knew about it? She had done the only thing she could do. She had left.

Now she worked in television and the same thing had happened again.

She had videotape, actual *videotape* of the most astounding story in the history of, well *anything*: a forgotten outpost of an alien civilization marooned on the outermost planet of our own solar system.

She had the story.

She had *been* there.

She had *seen* it.

She had the *videotape*, for God's sake.

And if she ever showed it to anybody, she would be a laughing stock.

How could she prove any of this? It wasn't even worth thinking about. The whole thing was a nightmare from virtually any angle she cared to look at it from. Her head was beginning to throb.

She had some aspirin in her bag. She went out of the little editing suite to the water dispenser down the corridor. She took the aspirin and drank several cups of water.

The place seemed to be very quiet. Usually there were more people bustling about the place, or at least *some* people bustling around the place. She popped her head round the door of the editing suite next to hers but there was no one there.

She had gone rather overboard keeping people out of her own suite. 'DO NOT DISTURB,' the notice read. 'DO NOT EVEN THINK OF ENTERING. I DON'T CARE WHAT IT IS. GO AWAY. I'M BUSY!'

When she went back in she noticed that the message light on her phone extension was winking, and wondered how long it had been on.

'Hello?' she said to the receptionist.

'Oh, Miss McMillan, I'm so glad you called. Everybody's been trying to reach you. Your TV company. They're desperate to reach you. Can you call them?'

'Why didn't you put them through?' said Tricia.

'You said I wasn't to put anybody through for anything. You said I was to deny that you were even here. I didn't know what to do. I came up to give you a message, but . . .'

'OK,' said Tricia, cursing herself. She phoned her office.

'*Tricia!* Where the haemorrhaging *fuck* are you?'

'At the editing—'

'They said—'

'I know. What's up?'

'What's *up*? Only a bloody alien spaceship!'

'What? *Where?'*

'Regent's Park. Big silver job. Some girl with a bird.

She speaks English and throws rocks at people and wants someone to repair her watch. Just get there.'

Tricia stared at it.

It wasn't a Grebulon ship. Not that she was suddenly an expert on extraterrestrial craft, but this was a sleek and beautiful silver and white thing about the size of a large ocean-going yacht, which is what it most resembled. Next to this, the structures of the huge half-dismantled Grebulon ship looked like gun turrets on a battleship. Gun turrets. That's what those blank grey buildings had looked like. And what was odd about them was that by the time she passed them again on her way to reboarding the small Grebulon craft, they had moved. These things flitted briefly through her head as she ran from the taxi to meet her camera crew.

'Where's the girl?' she shouted above the noise of helicopters and police sirens.

'There!' shouted the producer while the sound engineer hurried to clip a radio mike to her. 'She says her mother and father came from here in some parallel dimension or something like that, and she's got her father's watch, and . . . I don't know. What can I tell you? Busk it. Ask her what it feels like to be from outer space.'

'Thanks a lot, Ted,' muttered Tricia, checked that her mike was securely clipped, gave the engineer some level, took a deep breath, tossed her hair back and switched into her role of professional reporter, on home ground, ready for anything.

At least, nearly anything.

She turned to look for the girl. That must be her, with the wild hair and wild eyes. The girl turned towards her. And stared.

'Mother!' she screamed, and started to hurl rocks at Tricia.

22

Daylight exploded around them. Hot, heavy sun. A desert plain stretched out ahead in a haze of heat. They thundered out into it.

'Jump!' shouted Ford Prefect.

'What?' shouted Arthur Dent, holding on for dear life.

There was no reply.

'What did you say?' shouted Arthur again, and then realized that Ford Prefect was no longer there. He looked around in panic and started to slip. Realizing he couldn't hold on any longer he pushed himself sideways as hard as he could and rolled into a ball as he hit the ground, rolling, rolling away from the pounding hooves.

What a day, he thought, as he started furiously coughing dust up out of his lungs. He hadn't had a day as bad as this since the Earth had been blown up. He staggered up to his knees, and then up to his feet and started to run away. He didn't know what from or what to, but running away seemed a prudent move.

He ran straight into Ford Prefect, who was standing there surveying the scene.

'Look,' said Ford. 'That is precisely what we need.'

Arthur coughed up some more dust, and wiped some other dust out of his hair and eyes. He turned, panting, to look at what Ford was looking at.

It didn't look much like the domain of a King, or *the* King, or any kind of King. It looked quite inviting, though.

First, the context. This was a desert world. The dusty earth was packed hard and had neatly bruised every last bit of Arthur that hadn't already been bruised by the festivities of the previous night. Some way ahead of them were great cliffs that looked like sandstone, eroded by the wind and what little rain presumably fell in those parts into wild and fantastic shapes, which matched the fantastic shapes of the giant cacti that sprouted here and there from the arid, orange landscape.

For a moment Arthur dared to hope they had unexpectedly arrived in Arizona or New Mexico or maybe South Dakota, but there was plenty of evidence that this was not the case.

The Perfectly Normal Beasts were, for a start, still thundering, still pounding. They swept up in their tens of thousands from the far horizon, disappeared completely for about half a mile, then swept off, thundering and pounding to the distant horizon opposite.

Then there were the spaceships parked in front of the Bar & Grill. Ah. The Domain of the King Bar & Grill. Bit of an anti-climax, thought Arthur to himself.

In fact only one of the spaceships was parked in front of the Domain of the King Bar & Grill. The other three were in a parking lot by the side of the Bar & Grill. It was the one in front that caught the eye, though. Wonderful-looking thing. Wild fins all over it, far, far too much chrome all over the fins and most of the actual bodywork painted in a shocking pink. It crouched there like an immense brooding insect and looked as if it was at any moment about to jump on something about a mile away.

The Domain of the King Bar & Grill was slap bang in the middle of where the Perfectly Normal Beasts would be charging if they didn't take a minor transdimensional diversion on the way. It stood on its own, undisturbed. An ordinary Bar & Grill. A truckstop diner. Somewhere in the middle of nowhere. Quiet. The Domain of the King.

'Gonna buy that spaceship,' said Ford quietly.

'Buy it?' said Arthur. 'That's not like you. I thought you usually pinched them.'

'Sometimes you have to show a little respect,' said Ford.

'Probably have to show a little cash as well,' said Arthur. 'How the hell much is that thing worth?'

With a tiny movement, Ford brought his Dine-O-Charge credit card up out of his pocket. Arthur noticed that the hand holding it was trembling very slightly.

'I'll teach them to make me the restaurant critic . . .' breathed Ford.

'What do you mean?' asked Arthur.

'I'll show you,' said Ford with a nasty glint in his eye. 'Let's go and run up a few *expenses*, shall we?'

'Couple beers,' said Ford, 'and, I dunno, a couple bacon rolls, whatever you got, oh and that pink thing outside.'

He flipped his card on the top of the bar and looked around casually.

There was a kind of silence.

There hadn't been a lot of noise before, but there was definitely a kind of silence now. Even the distant thunder of the Perfectly Normal Beasts carefully avoiding the Domain of the King seemed suddenly a little muted.

'Just *rode* into town,' said Ford as if nothing was odd about that or about anything else. He was leaning against the bar at an extravagantly relaxed angle.

There were about three other customers in the place, sitting at tables, nursing beers. About three. Some people would say there were exactly three, but it wasn't that kind of a place, not the kind of a place that you felt like being that specific in. There was some big guy setting up some stuff on the little stage as well. Old drum kit. Couple guitars. Country and Western kind of stuff.

The barman was not moving very swiftly to get in Ford's order. In fact he wasn't moving at all.

'Not sure that the pink thing's for sale,' he said at last in the kind of accent that went on for quite a long time.

'Sure it is,' said Ford. 'How much you want?'

'Well . . .'

'Think of a number, I'll double it.'

'T'ain't mine to sell,' said the barman.

'So, whose?'

The barman nodded at the big guy setting up on the stage. Big fat guy, moving slow, balding.

Ford nodded. He grinned.

'OK,' he said. 'Get the beers, get the rolls. Keep the tab open.'

Arthur sat at the bar and rested. He was used to not knowing what was going on. He felt comfortable with it. The beer was pretty good and made him a little sleepy, which he didn't mind at all. The bacon rolls were not bacon rolls. They were Perfectly Normal Beast rolls. He exchanged a few professional roll-making remarks with the barman and just let Ford get on with whatever Ford wanted to do.

'OK,' said Ford, returning to his stool. 'It's cool. We got the pink thing.'

The barman was very surprised. 'He's selling it to you?'

'He's giving it to us for free,' said Ford, taking a gnaw at his roll. 'Hey, no, keep the tab open, though. We have some items to add to it. Good roll.'

He took a deep pull of beer.

'Good beer,' he added. 'Good ship, too,' he said, eyeing the big pink and chrome insect-like thing, bits of which could be seen through the windows of the bar. 'Good everything, pretty much. You know,' he said, sitting back, reflectively, 'it's at times like this that you kind of wonder if it's worth worrying about the fabric of space–time and the causal integrity of the multidimensional probability matrix and the potential collapse of all wave forms in the Whole Sort of General Mish Mash and all that sort of stuff that's been bugging me. Maybe I feel that what the big guy says is right. Just let it all go. What does it matter? Let it go.'

'Which big guy?' said Arthur.

Ford just nodded towards the stage. The big guy was saying 'one two' into the mike a couple of times. Couple other guys were on the stage now. Drums. Guitar.

The barman, who had been silent for a moment or two, said, 'You say he's letting you *have* his ship?'

'Yeah,' said Ford. 'Let it all go, is what he said. Take the ship. Take it with my blessing. Be good to her. I will be good to her.'

He took a pull at his beer again.

'Like I was saying,' he went on. 'It's at times like this that you kind of think, let it all go. But then you think of guys like InfiniDim Enterprises and you think, they are not going to get away with it. They are going to suffer. It is my sacred and holy duty to see those guys suffer. Here, let me put something on the tab for the singer. I asked for a special request and we agreed. It's to go on the tab. OK?'

'OK,' said the barman, cautiously. Then he shrugged. 'OK, however you want to do it. How much?'

Ford named a figure. The barman fell over amongst the bottles and glasses. Ford vaulted quickly over the bar to check that he was all right and help him back up to his feet. He'd cut his finger and his elbow a bit and was feeling a little woozy but was otherwise fine. The big guy started to sing. The barman hobbled off with Ford's credit card to get authorization.

'Is there stuff going on here that I don't know about?' said Arthur to Ford.

'Isn't there usually?' said Ford.

'No need to be like that,' said Arthur. He began to wake up. 'Shouldn't we be going?' he said suddenly. 'Will that ship get us to Earth?'

'Sure will,' said Ford.

'That's where Random will be going!' said Arthur with a start. 'We can follow her! But . . . er . . .'

Ford let Arthur get on with thinking things out for himself while he got out his old edition of *The Hitchhiker's Guide to the Galaxy.*

'But where are we on the probability axis thing?' said Arthur. 'Will the Earth be there or not there? I spent so much time looking for it. All I found was planets that were a bit like it or not at all like it, though it was clearly the right place because of the continents. The worst version was called NowWhat where I got bitten by some wretched little animal. That's how they communicated, you know, by biting each other. Bloody painful. Then half the time, of course, the Earth isn't even there because it's been blown up by the bloody Vogons. How much sense am I making?'

Ford didn't comment. He was listening to something. He passed the *Guide* over to Arthur and pointed at the screen. The active entry read: 'Earth. Mostly harmless.'

'You mean it's there!' said Arthur excitedly. 'The Earth is there! That's where Random will be going! The bird was showing her the Earth in the rainstorm!'

Ford motioned Arthur to shout a little less loudly. He was listening.

Arthur was growing impatient. He'd heard bar singers sing 'Love Me Tender' before. He was a bit surprised to hear it here, right in the middle of wherever the hell this was, certainly not Earth, but then things tended not to surprise him these days as much as formerly. The singer was quite good, as bar singers went, if you liked that sort of thing, but Arthur was getting fretful.

He glanced at his watch. This only served to remind him that he didn't have his watch any more. Random had it, or at least the remains of it.

'Don't you think we should be going?' he said, insistently.

'Shhh!' said Ford. 'I paid to hear this song.' He seemed to have tears in his eyes, which Arthur found a bit disturbing. He'd never seen Ford moved by anything other than very, very strong drink. Probably the dust. He waited, tapping his fingers irritably, out of time with the music.

The song ended. The singer went on to do 'Heartbreak Hotel'.

'Anyway,' Ford whispered, 'I've got to review the restaurant.'

'What?'

'I have to write a review.'

'Write a *review*? Of this place?'

'Filing the review validates the expenses claim. I've fixed it so that it happens completely automatically and untraceably. This bill is going to *need* some validation,' he added quietly, staring into his beer with a nasty smirk.

'For a couple of beers and a roll?'

'And a tip for the singer.'

'Why, how much did you tip him?'

Ford named a figure again.

'I don't know how much that is,' said Arthur. 'What's it worth in pounds sterling? What would it buy you?'

'It would probably buy you, roughly . . . er . . .' Ford screwed his eyes up as he did some calculations in his head. 'Switzerland,' he said at last. He picked up his *Hitchhiker's Guide* and started to type.

Arthur nodded intelligently. There were times when he wished he understood what on earth Ford was talking about, and other times, like now, when he felt it was probably safer not even to try. He looked over Ford's shoulder. 'This isn't going to take long, is it?' he said.

'Nah,' said Ford. 'Piece of piss. Just mention that the rolls were quite good, the beer good and cold, local wildlife nicely eccentric, the bar singer the best in the known universe, and that's about it. Doesn't need much. Just a validation.'

He touched an area on the screen marked ENTER and the message vanished into the Sub-Etha.

'You thought the singer was pretty good, then?'

'Yeah,' said Ford. The barman was returning with a piece of paper, which seemed to be trembling in his hand.

He pushed it over to Ford with a kind of nervous, reverential twitch.

'Funny thing,' said the barman. 'The system rejected it first couple times. Can't say it surprised me.' Beads of sweat were standing on his brow. 'Then suddenly it's, oh yeah, that's OK, and the system ... er, validates it. Just like that. You wanna ... sign it?'

Ford scanned the form quickly. He sucked his teeth. 'This is going to hurt InfiniDim a lot,' he said, with an appearance of concern. 'Oh well,' he added softly, 'screw 'em.'

He signed with a flourish and handed it back to the barman.

'More money,' he said, 'than the Colonel made for him in an entire career of doing crap movies and casino gigs. Just for doing what he does best. Standing up and singing in a bar. And he negotiated it himself. I think this is a good moment for him. Tell him I said thanks and buy him a drink.' He tossed a few coins on the bar. The barman pushed them away.

'I don't think that's necessary,' he said, slightly hoarsely.

'Tis to me,' said Ford. 'OK, we are outa here.'

They stood out in the heat and the dust and looked at the big pink and chrome thing with amazement and admiration. Or at least, Ford looked at it with amazement and admiration.

Arthur just looked at it. 'You don't think it's a bit overdone, do you?'

He said it again when they climbed inside it. The seats and quite a lot of the controls were covered in fine fur, skin or suede. There was a big gold monogram on the main control panel which just read 'EP'.

'You know,' said Ford as he fired up the ship's engines, 'I asked him if it was true that he had been abducted by aliens, and you know what he said?'

'Who?' said Arthur.

'The King.'

'Which King? Oh, we've had this conversation, haven't we?'

'Never mind,' said Ford. 'For what it's worth, he said, no. He went of his own accord.'

'I'm still not sure who we're talking about,' said Arthur.

Ford shook his head. 'Look,' he said, 'there are some tapes over in the compartment to your left. Why don't you choose some music and put it on?'

'OK,' said Arthur, and flipped through the cartons. 'Do you like Elvis Presley?' he said.

'Yeah I do, as a matter of fact,' said Ford. 'Now. I hope this machine can leap like it looks like it can.' He engaged the main drive.

'Yeeehaah!' shouted Ford as they shot upwards at face-tearing speed.

It could.

23

The news networks don't like this kind of thing. They regard it as a waste. An incontrovertible spaceship arrives out of nowhere in the middle of London and it is sensational news of the highest magnitude. Another completely different one arrives three and a half hours later and somehow it isn't.

'ANOTHER SPACECRAFT!' said the headlines and news-stand billboards. 'THIS ONE'S PINK.' A couple of months later they could have made a lot more of it. The third spacecraft, half an hour after that, the little four-berth Hrundi runabout, only made it on to the local news.

Ford and Arthur had come screaming down out of the stratosphere and parked neatly on Portland Place. It was just after six-thirty in the evening and there were spaces free. They mingled briefly with the crowd that gathered round to ogle, then said loudly that if no one else was going to call the police they would, and made good their escape.

'Home . . .' said Arthur, a husky tone creeping into his voice as he gazed, misty-eyed around him.

'Oh, don't get all maudlin on me,' snapped Ford. 'We have to find your daughter and we have to find that bird thing.'

'How?' said Arthur. 'This is a planet of five and a half billion people, and . . .'

'Yes,' said Ford. 'But only one of them has just arrived from outer space in a large silver spaceship accompanied by a mechanical bird. I suggest we just find a television and something to drink while we watch it. We need some serious room service.'

*

They checked into a large two-bedroomed suite at the Langham. Mysteriously, Ford's Dine-O-Charge card, issued on a planet over five thousand light-years away, seemed to present the hotel's computer with no problems.

Ford hit the phones straight away while Arthur attempted to locate the television.

'OK,' said Ford. 'I want to order up some margaritas, please. Couple of pitchers. Couple of Chef's salads. And as much foie gras as you've got. And also London Zoo.'

'She's on the news!' shouted Arthur from the next room.

'That's what I said,' said Ford into the phone. 'London Zoo. Just charge it to the room.'

'She's . . . Good God!' shouted Arthur. 'Do you know who she's being interviewed by?'

'Are you having difficulty understanding the English language?' continued Ford. 'It's the zoo just up the road from here. I don't care if it's closed this evening. I don't want to buy a ticket, I just want to buy the zoo. I don't care if you're busy. This is room service, I'm in a room and I want some service. Got a piece of paper? OK. Here's what I want you to do. All the animals that can be safely returned to the wild, return them. Set up some good teams of people to monitor their progress in the wild, see that they're doing OK.'

'It's *Trillian*!' shouted Arthur. 'Or is it . . . er . . . God, I can't stand all this parallel universe stuff. It's so bloody confusing. It seems to be a different Trillian. It's Tricia McMillan which is what Trillian used to be called before . . . er . . . Why don't you come and watch, see if you can figure it out?'

'Just a second,' Ford shouted, and returned to his negotiations with room service. 'Then we'll need some natural reserves for the animals that can't hack it in the wild,' he said. 'Set up a team to work out the best places to do that. We might need to buy somewhere like Zaïre and maybe some islands. Madagascar. Baffin. Sumatra. Those kind of places. We'll need a wide variety of habitats. Look, I don't see why you're seeing this as a problem. Learn to delegate. Hire whoever you want. Get on to it. I think you'll find my credit is good. And blue cheese dressing on the salad. Thank you.'

He put the phone down and went through to Arthur, who was sitting on the edge of his bed watching television.

'I ordered us some foie gras,' said Ford.

'What?' said Arthur, whose attention was entirely focused on the television.

'I said I ordered us some foie gras.'

'Oh,' said Arthur, vaguely. 'Um, I always feel a bit bad about foie gras. Bit cruel to the geese, isn't it?'

'Fuck 'em,' said Ford, slumping on the bed. 'You can't care about every damn thing.'

'Well, that's all very well for you to say, but . . .'

'Drop it!' said Ford. 'If you don't like it I'll have yours. What's happening?'

'Chaos!' said Arthur. 'Complete chaos! Random keeps on screaming at Trillian, or Tricia or whoever it is, that she abandoned her and then demanding to go to a good night club. Tricia's broken down in tears and says she's never even met Random let alone given birth to her. Then she suddenly started howling about someone called Rupert and said that he had lost his mind or something. I didn't quite follow that bit, to be honest. Then Random started throwing stuff and they've cut to a commercial break while they try and sort it all out. Oh! They've just cut back to the studio! Shut up and watch.'

A rather shaken anchorman appeared on the screen and apologized to viewers for the disruption of the previous item. He said he didn't have any very clear news to report, only that the mysterious girl, who called herself Random Frequent Flyer Dent, had left the studio to, er, rest. Tricia McMillan would be, he hoped, back tomorrow. Meanwhile, fresh reports of UFO activity were coming in . . .

Ford leaped up off the bed, grabbed the nearest phone and jabbed at a number.

'Concierge? You want to own the hotel? It's yours if you can find out for me in five minutes which clubs Tricia McMillan belongs to. Just charge the whole thing to this room.'

24

Away in the inky depths of space invisible movements were being made.

Invisible to any of the inhabitants of the strange and temperamental Plural zone at the focus of which lay the infinitely multitudinous possibilities of the planet called Earth, but not inconsequential to them.

At the very edge of the solar system, hunkered down on a green leatherette sofa, staring fretfully at a range of TV and computer screens, sat a very worried Grebulon leader. He was fiddling with stuff. Fiddling with his book on astrology. Fiddling with the console of his computer. Fiddling with the displays being fed through to him constantly from all of the Grebulons' monitoring devices, all of them focused on the planet Earth.

He was distressed. Their mission was to monitor. But

to monitor secretly. He was a bit fed up with his mission, to be honest. He was fairly certain that his mission must have been to do more than sit around watching TV for years on end. They certainly had a lot of other equipment with them that must have had some purpose if only they hadn't accidentally lost all trace of their purpose. He needed a sense of purpose in life, which was why he had turned to astrology to fill the yawning gulf that existed in the middle of his mind and soul. That would tell him something, surely.

Well, it was telling him something.

It was telling him, as far as he could make out, that he was about to have a very bad month, that things were going to go from bad to worse if he didn't get a grip on things and start making some positive moves and thinking things out for himself.

It was true. It was very clear from his star chart which he had worked out using his astrology book and the computer program which that nice Tricia McMillan had designed for him to re-triangulate all the appropriate astronomical data. Earth-based astrology had to be entirely recalculated to yield results that were meaningful to the Grebulons here on the tenth planet out on the frozen edges of the solar system.

The recalculations showed absolutely clearly and unambiguously that he was going to have a very bad month indeed, starting with today. Because today Earth was starting to rise into Capricorn, and that, for the Grebulon leader, who showed all the character signs of being a classic Taurus, was very bad indeed.

Now was the time, his horoscope said, for taking positive actions, making tough decisions, seeing what needed to be done and doing it. This was all very difficult for him, but he knew that nobody ever said that doing tough stuff wasn't tough. The computer was already tracking and predicting the second-by-second location of the planet Earth. He ordered the great grey turrets to swivel.

Because all of the Grebulon surveillance equipment was focused on the planet Earth, it failed to spot that there was now another source of data in the solar system.

Its chances of spotting this other source of data – a massive yellow constructor ship – accidentally were practically nil. It was as far from the sun as Rupert was, but almost diametrically opposite, almost hidden by the sun.

Almost.

The massive yellow constructor ship wanted to be able to monitor events on Planet Ten without being spotted itself. It had managed this very successfully.

There were all sorts of other ways in which this ship was diametrically opposite to the Grebulons.

Its leader, its captain, had a very clear idea of what his purpose was. It was a very simple and plain one and he had been pursuing it in his simple, plain way for a considerable period of time now.

Anyone who knew of his purpose might have said that it was a pointless and ugly one, that it wasn't the sort of purpose that enhanced a life, put a spring in a person's step, made birds sing and flowers bloom. Rather the reverse, in fact. Absolutely the reverse.

It wasn't his job to worry about that, though. It was his job to do his job, which was to do his job. If that led to a certain narrowness of vision and circularity of thought then it wasn't his job to worry about such things. Any such things that came his way were referred to others who had, in turn, other people to refer such things to.

Many, many light-years from here, indeed from anywhere, lies the grim and long-abandoned planet, Vogsphere. Somewhere on a fetid, fog-bound mud bank on this planet there stands, surrounded by the dirty, broken and empty carapaces of the last few jewelled scuttling crabs, a small stone monument which marks the place where, it is thought, the species *Vogon vogonblurtus* first arose. On the monument there is carved an arrow which points away into the fog, under which are inscribed in plain, simple letters the words 'The buck stops there.'

Deep in the bowels of his unsightly yellow ship, the Vogon captain grunted as he reached for a slightly faded and dog-eared piece of paper that lay in front of him. A demolition order.

If you were to unravel exactly where the captain's job, which was to do his job which was to do his job, actually began, then it all came down at last to this piece of paper that had been issued to him by his immediate superior long ago. The piece of paper had an instruction on it, and his purpose was to carry out that instruction and put a little tick mark in the adjacent box when he had carried it out.

He had carried out the instruction once before, but a number of troublesome circumstances had prevented him from being able to put the tick in the little box.

One of the troublesome circumstances was the Plural nature of this Galactic sector, where the possible continually interfered with the probable. Simple demolition didn't get you any further than pushing down a bubble under a badly hung strip of wallpaper. Anything you demolished kept on popping up again. That would soon be taken care of.

Another was a small bunch of people who continually refused to be where they were supposed to be when they were supposed to be there. That, also, would soon be taken care of.

The third was an irritating and anarchic little device

called *The Hitchhiker's Guide to the Galaxy*. That was now well and truly taken care of and, in fact, through the phenomenal power of temporal reverse engineering, it was now itself the agency through which everything else would be taken care of. The captain had merely come to watch the final act of this drama. He himself did not have to lift a finger.

'Show me,' he said.

The shadowy shape of a bird spread its wings and rose into the air near him. Darkness engulfed the bridge. Dim lights danced briefly in the black eyes of the bird as, deep in its instructional address space, bracket after bracket was finally closing, if-clauses were finally ending, repeat loops halting, recursive functions calling themselves for the last few times.

A brilliant vision lit up in the darkness, a watery blue and green vision, a tube flowing through the air, shaped like a chopped-up string of sausages.

With a flatulent noise of satisfaction, the Vogon captain sat back to watch.

25

'Just there, number forty-two,' shouted Ford Prefect to the taxi-driver. 'Right here!'

The taxi lurched to a halt, and Ford and Arthur jumped out. They had stopped at quite a number of cash-dispensers on the way, and Ford chucked a fistful of money through the window at the driver.

The entrance to the club was dark, smart and severe. Only the smallest little plaque bore its name. Members knew where it was, and if you weren't a member then knowing where it was wasn't any help to you.

Ford Prefect was not a member of Stavro's though he had once been to Stavro's other club in New York. He had a very simple method of dealing with establishments of which he was not a member. He simply swept in as soon as the door was opened, pointed back at Arthur and said, 'It's OK, he's with me.'

He bounded down the dark glossy stairs, feeling very froody in his new shoes. They were suede and they were blue, and he was very pleased that in spite of everything else going on he had been sharp-eyed enough to spot them in a shop window from the back of a speeding taxi.

'I thought I told you not to come here.'

'What?' said Ford.

A thin, ill-looking man wearing something baggy and Italian was walking up the stairs past them, lighting a cigarette, and had stopped, suddenly.

'Not you,' he said. 'Him.'

He looked straight at Arthur, then seemed to become a little confused.

'Excuse me,' he said. 'I think I must have mistaken you for someone else.' He started on up the stairs again, but almost immediately turned round once more, even more puzzled. He stared at Arthur.

'Now what?' said Ford.

'What did you say?'

'I said, now what?' repeated Ford irritably.

'Yes, I think so,' said the man and swayed slightly and dropped the book of matches he'd been carrying. His mouth moved weakly. Then he put his hand to his forehead.

'Excuse me,' he said, 'I'm trying desperately to remember which drug I've just taken, but it must be one of those ones which mean you can't remember.'

He shook his head and turned away again, and went up towards the men's room.

'Come on,' said Ford. He hurried on downstairs, with Arthur following nervously in his wake. The encounter had shaken him badly and he didn't know why.

He didn't like places like this. For all of the dreams of Earth and home he had had for years, he now badly missed his hut on Lamuella with his knives and his sandwiches. He even missed Old Thrashbarg.

'Arthur!'

It was the most astounding effect. His name was being shouted in stereo.

He twisted to look one way. Up the stairs behind him he saw Trillian hurrying down towards him in her wonderfully rumpled Rymplon™. She was looking suddenly aghast.

He twisted the other way to see what she was looking suddenly aghast at.

At the bottom of the stairs was Trillian, wearing ... No – this was Tricia. Tricia that he had just seen, hysterical with confusion, on television. And behind her was Random, looking more wild-eyed than ever. Behind her in the recesses of the smart, dimly lit club, the other clientele of the evening formed a frozen tableau, staring anxiously up at the confrontation on the stairs.

For a few seconds everyone stood stock still. Only the music from behind the bar didn't know to stop throbbing.

'The gun she is holding,' said Ford quietly, nodding slightly towards Random, 'is a Wabanatta 3. It was in the ship she stole from me. It's quite dangerous, in fact. Just don't move for a moment. Let's just everybody stay calm and find out what's upsetting her.'

'Where do I *fit*?' screamed Random suddenly. The hand holding the gun was trembling fiercely. Her other hand delved into her pocket and pulled out the remains of Arthur's watch. She shook it at them.

'I thought I would fit here,' she cried, 'on the world

that made me! But it turns out that even my *mother* doesn't know who I am!' She flung the watch violently aside, and it smashed into the glasses behind the bar, scattering its innards.

Everyone was very quiet for a moment or two longer.

'Random,' said Trillian quietly from up on the stairs.

'Shut *up*!' shouted Random. 'You abandoned me!'

'Random, it is very important that you listen to me and understand,' persisted Trillian quietly. 'There isn't very much time. We must leave. We must all leave.'

'What are you talking about? We're always *leaving*!' She had both hands on the gun now, and both were shaking. There was no one in particular she was pointing it at. She was just pointing it at the world in general.

'Listen,' said Trillian again. 'I left you because I went to cover a war for the network. It was extremely dangerous. At least, I thought it was going to be. I arrived and the war had suddenly ceased to happen. There was a time anomaly and . . . listen! Please listen! A reconnaissance battleship had failed to turn up, the rest of the fleet was scattered in some farcical disarray. It's happening all the time now.'

'I don't care! I don't want to hear about your bloody *job*!' shouted Random. 'I want a home! I want to fit somewhere!'

'This is not your home,' said Trillian, still keeping her voice calm. 'You don't have one. We none of us have one. Hardly anybody has one any more. The missing ship I was just talking about. The people of that ship don't have a home. They don't know where they are from. They don't even have any memory of who they are or what they are for. They are very lost and very confused and very frightened. They are here in this solar system, and they are about to do something very . . . misguided because they are so lost and confused. We . . . must . . . leave . . . now. I can't tell you where there is to go to. Perhaps there isn't anywhere. But here is not the place to be. Please. One more time. Can we go?'

Random was wavering in panic and confusion.

'It's all right,' said Arthur gently. 'If I'm here, we're safe. Don't ask me to explain just now, but I am safe, so you are safe. OK?'

'What are you saying?' said Trillian.

'Let's all just relax,' said Arthur. He was feeling very tranquil. His life was charmed and none of this seemed real.

Slowly, gradually, Random began to relax, and to let the gun down, inch by inch.

Two things happened simultaneously.

The door to the men's room at the top of the stairs opened, and the man who had accosted Arthur came out, sniffing.

Startled at the sudden movement, Random lifted the gun again just as a man standing behind her made a grab for it.

Arthur threw himself forward. There was a deafening explosion. He fell awkwardly as Trillian threw herself down over him. The noise died away. Arthur looked up to see the man at the top of the stairs gazing down at him with a look of utter stupefaction.

'You . . .' he said. Then slowly, horribly, he fell apart.

Random threw the gun down and fell to her knees, sobbing. 'I'm sorry!' she said. 'I'm so sorry! I'm so, so sorry . . .'

Tricia went to her. Trillian went to her.

Arthur sat on the stairs with his head between his hands and had not the faintest idea what to do. Ford was sitting on the stair beneath him. He picked something up, looked at it with interest, and passed it up to Arthur.

'This mean anything to you?' he said.

Arthur took it. It was the book of matches which the dead man had dropped. It had the name of the club on it. It had the name of the proprietor of the club on it. It looked like this:

STAVRO MUELLER

BETA

He stared at it for some time as things began slowly to reassemble themselves in his mind. He wondered what he should do, but he only wondered it idly. Around him people were beginning to rush and shout a lot, but it was suddenly very clear to him that there was nothing to be done, not now or ever. Through the new strangeness of noise and light he could just make out the shape of Ford Prefect sitting back and laughing wildly.

A tremendous feeling of peace came over him. He knew that at last, for once and for ever, it was now all, finally, over.

In the darkness of the bridge at the heart of the Vogon ship, Prostetnic Vogon Jeltz sat alone. Lights flared briefly across the external vision screens that lined one wall. In the air above him the discontinuities in the blue and green watery sausage shape resolved themselves. Options collapsed, possibilities folded into each other, and the whole at last resolved itself out of existence.

A very deep darkness descended. The Vogon captain sat immersed in it for a few seconds.

'Light,' he said.

There was no response. The bird, too, had crumpled out of all possibility.

The Vogon turned on the light himself. He picked up

the piece of paper again and placed a little tick in the little box.

Well, that was done. His ship slunk off into the inky void.

In spite of having taken what he regarded as an extremely positive piece of action, the Grebulon Leader ended up having a very bad month after all. It was pretty much the same as all the previous months except that there was now nothing on the television any more. He put on a little light music instead.